T0207946

LAURA E. FEDERMEYER

WestBow Press books may be ordered through booksellers or by contacting:

WestBow Press
A Division of Thomas Nelson
1663 Liberty Drive
Bloomington, IN 47403
www.westbowpress.com
1 (866) 928-1240



ISBN: 978-1-4908-1933-4 (sc)

Library of Congrsss Control Number: 2013922395

Printed in the United States of America.

WestBow Press rev. date: 12/23/2013

# *My Dedication*

I would like to dedicate this book, first to my Savior who gave me the talent and inspiration to write. My Church friends, especially Glenda who encouraged me to keep writing and Marion who helped Glenda proof-read my story. Also, my husband, Richard, who stood behind me with his encouragement.

# CONTENTS

# CHAPTER 1

Loren was bored. The white velvet wing-backed chair where she sat near the patio doorway was getting uncomfortable. She didn't remember how long she had been sitting there staring at all the people in the room and not really seeing them. She could hear the clink of their glasses as they freely drank the champagne offered to them by the waiters. Her back started to itch. Uncut threads on the sequences on the back of her newly purchased dress seemed to be causing the problem. Did she dare wiggle to get comfortable? In a nervous action, she crossed her slim legs and tugged down the gown's long skirt to cover them again. Suddenly she had the urge to twiddle her thumbs like she used to do when she was young. Her lips twitched with a half smile just thinking about doing it. People in her parent's social group were everywhere. It was almost a standing room only. Bodies bumped against each other, their colognes and perfumes mixing together along with the cigarette and cigar smoke.

The loud laughter of the guests was getting irritating to Loren's ears.

Everyone was dressed in the latest fashions; as they all tried to outdo one another. Someone was getting married and this was the excuse to have a party. Loren snorted. Married. What was so good about being married to the same person for hundreds of years? She had seen marriages come and go. Her parents had divorced and remarried, not once, but twice. None that she knew of was a lifetime venture.

Single life had more of an appeal to her. She was twenty-five and in no hurry to be saddled with a couple of screaming rug-rats or to the task of changing dirty diapers. Her five foot six inch figure was in perfect shape. Several trips to the spa during the week helped keep her strong and lithe. Through all her many interests and hobbies, she wanted to keep in shape. Loren had skydived, skied the roughest snow slopes, and now her new diversion from boredom was horseback riding. Once she mastered the balance and control of the horse, she planned to take an all day ride with other riders and a guide into the mountain range.

She absentmindedly touched her coffered dark brown hair, that had been twisted into a bun. Chocolate brown eyes stared out over the crowd not really seeing anything or anyone she liked. The make-up she wore hid the sprinkle of freckles across her nose. Dangling diamond earrings sparkled in her ears as they swayed with her every head movement. Loren watched the well dressed young men gathered around the groom to be. The women her age were in another corner probably talking about the men.

Loren saw how they stole glances over at the men, then quickly turned back to the other women. She really should be with them, she thought. Even though the chair was getting uncomfortable, she wiggled around in it and stayed seated. She let her thoughts drift to an incident that happened a week ago. Everything around her was momentarily quiet.

A young preacher had approached her on the street one day last week and spoke to her about Jesus Christ. Loren had only heard that name mentioned when a person was mad and swore. The preacher had raised so much of her curiosity that she wanted to know more. He had mentioned attending church. The preacher had told her about a peace that only God could give to her. The Bible was God's Word. She could find everything in there that she needed to know about God and His

Son Jesus. Happiness and peace of mind. Could she really obtain that? Truly she wouldn't find it here, tonight. Her so-called friends would soon be drunk and disorderly. Not pleasant to be around since she didn't drink. Loren breathed in deeply, then coughed. In her daydreaming thoughts, she had forgotten the guests were also smoking. Slowly she glanced around the room. The guests voices were droning on louder as the evening progressed. If she sat there much longer, she would get a real headache. Near the ceiling was the tell-tale signs of the smoky cloud. The heavy wine colored drapes would soon hold all that smoke and become discolored. Gracefully she stood up. Stretching, she flexed her stiffening muscles. Loren moved forward in the full length light green gown.

As it swirled about her legs, she was careful not to trip in her high heels. No one paid any attention to her as she walked toward the patio door. In fact, the whole scene before her was becoming old. Outside she could breathe fresh air and think.

The smells of the garden beyond the patio assailed her nose as she opened the glass doors. A well kept rose garden spread out beyond the patio stones for guests to enjoy in a brief walk through. Quietly she closed the patio door behind her and walked over to the railing. Her hands laid on the cold railing feeling the roughness of the concrete. Looking down at her hands, she stared at the long tapered fingers with the light red painted nails. Her whole life at that moment seemed depressing. She didn't have a vocation or a job to keep her busy every day. Her parents had servants at their beck and call so Loren had no to work to do. Daily servants made her bed and hung up her clothes in her huge walk in closet. Her money from her parents had kept her supposedly happy all these years since college.

A sound of the patio door opening caused her to slowly turn back toward the house. She pressed her back up against the cold concrete wall. Jeremy, a banker's son, came through the door, dressed in a camel tan tailored suit of that made him the envy of all the women present. Attending a gym on a regular basis, he kept his body in excellent shape. His blonde hair curled slightly around his ears was held in place by a thick coating of hair spray. No one was allowed to touch it without permission.

Jeremy was vain and conceited. He toyed with women and gambled on anything else he thought he could win money on. Loren was ripe for the picking. His pale blue eyes hungrily looked her over from head to toe. Now was his chance. His words must be well chosen, for she was considered really hard to get. He had wanted her for a long time but was never in her good graces. Now that he had her all alone, he could make a play for her affections. Moving like a cat on the prowl, he came closer and stood over her.

Loren smelled the alcohol on his breath and the faint traces of cigar smoke on his clothes.

Being a lady, she awaited for him to speak first. She put on her best smile and waited.

"Loren, my dear, how have you been?"

"Quite well, Jeremy. And you?"

"When are you going to let me show you around and maybe go out for dinner?"

"I've been rather busy." lied Loren. "I am taking riding lessons now."

Jeremy wrinkled his nose. "All that smell of horse manure! How can you stand it?"

Loren chuckled. "We really don't smell it much. The horses are saddled when we get there for our lesson. I don't go into the barn. It does look fairly clean, though. You don't like horses?"

"When they are running and the horse that I have money on is in the lead, yes."

"Have you won very much?"

Jeremy shook his head. "No, but it is fun watching them try. It's the feel you get from the racing. The crowd cheering and you just normally get caught up in all the excitement. Maybe you would like to go with me to the track tomorrow?"

He watched the expressions on her face knowing that she would go, because of her curiosity. He had known Loren for a long time and had studied her numerous times. He had liked what he saw, but she had avoided all attempts to become friends or even acquaintances. She had this little habit of chewing on her lower lip when she was really thinking, that drove him to want to kiss her. She was so desirable! Loren finally nodded slowly. She had never been to a horse race. This might be another avenue of distraction for her. He put his hands on her bare shoulders and started to pull her towards him.

Instantly she pulled back. He had forgotten that some men referred her to the 'Ice Princess' an untouchable female. He would have to take it slowly with her. If his patience would allow, he would soon conquer the 'Ice Princess'. Quickly he apologized. He dropped his arms to his sides.

"Sorry, Loren. I was just excited that you had agreed to go with me. I'll pick you up at ten and we can have lunch at the clubhouse. I have front row seats in the air conditioned section. We can eat and watch the horses run at the same time."

"All right. See you tomorrow." She turned to go back inside leaving him there by the railing. When she reached the door, he had come up behind her and opened the door for her. His arm brushed the back of her shoulders. Inwardly she cringed. Gritting her teeth, she endured the touch as she glided inside the room. Guests were leaving or venturing off into other parts of the house. She heard someone laughing from the stairwell and wondered what anyone would be doing upstairs. Her neck turned red as she remembered what couples did in the bedrooms. She whispered an 'Oh boy' as she headed for the front door. Jeremy was waiting at the door, holding her coat open as she slipped it on. With his free hand, he pushed open the door. With a wink and a smile, he nodded farewell.

Once behind the wheel of her car, she put her head down on the steering wheel. Breathing a sigh of relief that the evening was over, she straightened and put the key in the ignition. Tomorrow would be a new experience to test and add to her activities.

The party was soon out of her mind as she drove home with the windows down in the car. Cool night air blew in erasing some of the smoky smell from her gown. She had never understood why anyone would want to smoke or drink for that manner. Her new stepmother did both, but not much inside the house. She usually went out on their patio. Her father only drank socially, sometimes when he was at the club after playing a round of golf. She was closer to her father than her step mom. They had done lots of things together as she was growing up. Now, as an adult, he seemed to be a little distant. She was an independent lady, doing her own 'thing'. Her grades in school and college were at the top of her class. Her motivation was almost nil. She had all the money and servants to do the work for her. Loren never learned to sew or cook or even clean house. Not good wife material. Even to put on a party would be a big job for her on her own. No, she was just a little rich girl with lots of time on her hands.

Loren drove her little sports car into the three car garage and stepped out. One of the servants was there to hold the door to the house for her. She nodded her thanks and swept by him heading directly to her section of the house. It was late. Her maid Janet was waiting near her bedroom door to help put away the evening gown. She had already laid out Loren's evening nightgown with the bedcovers laid down. Janet helped her unzip the back and the dress slid to the floor. Loren stepped out and walked to the adjoining bathroom. A nice long hot shower helped to erase more of the smoky smell, from the party. In her stepmother's room, there were what people called bar room plants that absorbed the smoke from cigarettes. Other sprays were used to help them along. In Loren's part of the house, no smoke smell reached her doors.

Now, with a big fluffy towel wrapped around her, she went back into the bedroom and began her bedtime ritual. Already her thoughts were on the next day and what she would encounter at the racetrack. Would it be exciting to watch horses run against each other? Just thinking about when she would be good enough to ride that well excited her. With the last brush stroke through her hair, she got up and climbed under the covers. Reaching over with one hand, she flipped off the light. With a soft moan of pleasure, Loren rested her head on the pillow and went to sleep.

# CHAPTER 2

Saturday morning was turning out to be a wonderful day. The sun was shining and with just enough breeze to make the day bearable. Loren was ready when Jeremy drove up in his Mercedes convertible. She carried a silk scarf to put on her head to keep her hair from blowing all over. She had anticipated him having the top down. Loren knew his character, too. She could almost anticipate his every move and sometimes guess what kind of a mood he was in. He was out of the car and quickly around to the other side to open the car door for her. A gentleman's gentleman. She put on the scarf and tied it securely under her chin as he put the car in gear and drove down the driveway.

At the clubhouse, everyone greeted them. Some had a surprised look on their faces to see Loren with Jeremy, but didn't make any comment in front of them. Loren nodded to everyone in greeting as they weaved their way through the tables. Jeremy held out her chair as she sat down. Far below people were gathering in the stands to watch the races. Loren looked over the crowd and then back around the restaurant.

People of all ages and dress were milling about below them. The adults carried programs about the races, horses and what their standings were. A couple of tractors were on the track smoothing the dirt into place. Even though no horses were on the track, Loren began to feel the excitement building within her. She visualized herself as a jockey riding on one of the powerful mounts. The horse that she was riding on at her lessons was long legged and muscular. She had felt the excitement of being on its back with its powerful muscles moving as they worked in the corral. She was anticipating the time when she could run the horse. Right now, she was walking, trotting and just generally trying to keep upright in the saddle. She had chosen a western saddle equipped with a horn and cantle for a more secure seat.

A waiter appeared at their table and gave them menus. Loren looked over the many choices and chose her entrée. Full ice tea glasses were set before them. Loren turned her attention back to her escort. Jeremy wore a white knit top with tan slacks. His hair, like always, was perfectly in place. She wondered what women would do with all that thick hairspray in their fingers after touching his head. Would he even ask her to get that close and allow her the privilege of touching it? She shook her head slightly to clear the thought. Even the thought of doing it gave her the willies.

Jeremy turned his aristocratic nose back around from his scanning of a new woman sitting at a table near the window overlooking the track to look at Loren. She could easily hold a candle to a stranger. If Loren would ever let him get close enough to her. He sighed. Would the chase for her affection be worth it in the long run?

Already he could tell she was distracted by something else. Maybe she was thinking about being intimate with him! His heart jumped a beat. Licking his dry lips, he turned his full attention on Loren.

"Loren, what do you think so far?"

"It is all so amazing! I can feel the excitement all around me and the horses are not even out of the barn. Can we go trackside after a couple races up here for a closer view?"

Jeremy wrinkled his nose at the thought of all the dirt, dust and being around common people. He gave her one of his winning smiles anyhow. "Sure. I believe they have ten races planned. We can watch four or five up here and go down. We'll want to leave before the last race to beat the traffic."

Once their meal was brought to them, they began eating slowly. The first race wouldn't start for another thirty minutes. Where their seats were located was only a few rooms and stairways away. The clubhouse where they sat now was above the enclosed section for high society to sit in comfort.

Loren dabbed the cloth napkin across her mouth. The crab and shrimp salad had been delicious, the desert, a chocolate mousse made the meal perfect. She smiled over at Jeremy. "Thank you for the wonderful meal. The food was superb."

"The restaurant is open now until winter. We can come back again if you like."

"We'll see."

Jeremy grinned. It was going to be fun trying to win her. He had two points in his favor for now. She liked the good food and the new exciting activity soon to unfold. He stood up and moved to help her out of her chair. He glanced over toward the other woman's table and received a nod in recognition. Loren stood up and Jeremy gently put his hand on her back to steer her toward the doorway leading to the enclosed grandstand.

He purposely passed the woman's table where she stuck a slip of paper into his hand. Grinning to himself, he knew it held the phone number and her name. If he struck out with Loren, then well……

Jeremy picked up a program and followed Loren to their seats. Just one glance at her told him she was excited. Would she stay that way and want more? He knew how easily it was for her to become bored with the mundane daily duties. He sometimes worked at the bank, but she didn't do anything really useful. He wasn't jealous either. He liked being in the bank and helping people invest their money. He was good at manipulating people to spend their money. He had done well for his customers as well as himself in the stock market. All the new clothes in his closet and the new Mercedes was evident of his good luck in his investing.

The bugle began to blow signaling that the horses for the first race were on their way from the barn. From where they sat, everything could be seen without someone's head in the way. Loren watched anxiously as the first horse walked onto the track. She thrilled at the many bright colors of the jockey's clothing. They were so small! How could they manage such huge beasts?

Loren wiggled around in her seat to get a better view of the next horse and jockey. The second horse was a magnificent black. It pranced and tossed its head giving the jockey all he could manage to keep it in line with the others. When all ten horses were out on the track, Jeremy leaned over close.

"Do you see anyone you would risk a couple of dollars on?"

"Well, I like the looks of the number 2 horse. He is really anxious to run."

Jeremy checked the program. The horse had a 24-1 chance to win. He frowned some and gave Loren a crooked grin. "He's not really a favorite. He would be a long shot at best. I think the number four horse looks good."

It was Loren's turn to wrinkle up her nose at his choice. She had not been impressed by the number four. The horse moved sluggishly and the jockey looked like he was half asleep.

"How do you bet?" she asked, taking out her purse. Jeremy waved her off. He pulled his own billfold out and peeled off several bills.

"Let me do this your first time. Be right back." Jeremy got up and walked rapidly back to the betting windows. He would bet his horse and put a couple dollars on her number two. The horses were approaching the starting gate when he returned to his seat. He handed Loren her ticket. "I put ten dollars on his nose to win."

She smiled at him and turned her full attention back to the track. A bell sounded and the horses leaped out of the starting gate. She could almost feel the surge of power as the horses began heading for the first turn. Her choice was near the front.

Unknown to her, she was leaning forward in her seat and clutching her purse in a tight grip. Her black horse was staying near the front of the pack.

As they came around the last turn, some of the horses in the middle of the pack seemed to get their second wind. Several in the middle began passing leaders and were soon in the front. Loren's pick surged out in front and stayed there. Jeremy's pick was coming in almost dead last. He didn't get mad this time because he was getting his thrill from watching Loren. Her face was shining and her eyes sparkling. She was even breathing hard. Was she actually feeling the ride herself? She raised both hands high as the number two horse was declared the winner. She looked over at Jeremy. She felt her cheeks turn red.

"Did I really win?"

Jeremy laughed. "Well your horse pick did. Were you pretending to ride the horse yourself?"

Loren laughed. "I think I was. I'm all out of breath. You'll get your ten dollars back."

Jeremy shook his head. "A lot more than that, darlin'. That horse was not even supposed to come in third, let alone first. Did you see where my pick came in? That is where according to the statistics, is where your horse was supposed to be."

Loren laughed again. "Well, your horse and rider looked like they had taken a dose of sleeping pills. I think I could have beaten it in a foot race."

"Are you enjoying yourself?"

"Yes. Do they race every Saturday?"

"They will until the season is over for the winter. Did you want to make this a weekly event in your social calendar?"

"We'll see. Oh, they are calling the horses for the next race." Loren turned her attention back to the track. New horses and riders were coming out.

She looked all of them over carefully, then silently chose one to win. This was fun. She was actually enjoying herself. By the looks on some of the other people there, they seemed to be concerned about their losing. How much were they betting on their pick? Were they betting every race? She didn't want to get hooked on this sport. It required lots of money and she didn't want to spend it foolishly. They were fun to watch, but people needed to keep their money in their pocket or bank.

After three races, Loren excused herself to go to the ladies lounge. As she entered the lounge, the first room was decorated with cream colored wallpaper accented by small flowers of some sort. Placed along the wall were comfortable chairs, mirrors and even a table set up with coffee and donuts. She glanced over at another table that held several women's magazines and a couple of books. Loren wondered what the women wanted with all of this when there were horses and races to watch. The thought then hit her. Some of the women were probably bored with their men or husbands watching the horses.

As her eyes swept over the neatly stacked magazines, she spotted a burgundy colored book sitting almost hidden in the upper right hand corner of the table.

Curious, she uncovered it and saw that it said Holy Bible on the cover. Instantly her thoughts went back to the young preacher on the street. This was God's Word! Forgetting what she had come in there for, she sat down in a chair beside the table. Almost reverently she picked up the Bible.

Inside the cover, someone had put a picture of Jesus holding a small white lamb. He was standing on what looked like a ledge with a mountain range all around.

The place looked dangerous and no place for a little defenseless lamb. Loren smiled at the memory of a white lamb. She had been seven or eight when her parents had taken her to a fair. There she had seen the baby animals and lambs in the petting zoo.

She remembered the story of Mary Had A Little Lamb and the lamb that followed Mary wherever she went. Well, she had tried to get her dad to get her a lamb so she could have one follow her around at home. They had lived near enough to the city where farm animals were forbidden. After the lamb incident, a puppy had shown up at their home. The puppy replaced the lamb and followed her around instead of a white lamb.

Loren wondered where the story was in the Bible. She leaved through several pages and then turned to the back. She found the word 'lamb' and sought out the references. This Book was so strange to her that she spent almost too much time in her searching. Using the index in the front, she found the scripture in Matthew 18:11-13 referring to the lamb.

As she read, she wondered why Jesus would look for one lamb when he already had ninety nine.

Tears formed in her eyes when she read the part of where He had found it. The picture in the front of the Bible was true. The lamb would not have survived on the sharp cliffs in the mountainside alone if Jesus had not rescued it. Loren wiped the tears from her eyes. Someone else came into the room about then and walked on past her toward the other door to the restroom stalls. Loren jerked back to the present. Looking at her watch, she realized that she had been in there way too long.

Jeremy would be concerned. She placed the Bible back on the table and walked into the back.

Jeremy had not really missed Loren. He had joined the other woman at her table several tables over and was planning to see her the next day. He was aware of Loren, though, and kept looking over toward the Woman's Lounge door. He tried to relax in the lady's company. She could tell he was distracted and knew she could get him eventually.

She had seen the 'other' woman and knew she had nothing on her. She was well skilled in 'reeling' in a man that she wanted. If they did not possess money to make her happy or jump to bid her every whims, then they were cast aside. She gave Jeremy her winning smile and rubbed her slim hand up his arm. Her long fingernails lightly brushing his arm. He felt good. He had made another conquest.

"Later, Jeremy. Call me." she practically purred.

"I will later tonight. This lady needs more time than I have to wait."

"Until later, then."

Jeremy easily got to his feet and returned to his table. Loren was just emerging from the Woman's Lounge. He saw her weak smile and wondered if something had happened. He stood and walked around the table to pull her chair out for her.

"Are you okay, Loren?"

Loren nodded and tried to focus back on the racetrack where horses were once more walking onto the track. She wanted to know more about this man Jesus. He had risked His life to save one poor little helpless lamb. Did He do that for people? She must find out more. Her thoughts suddenly went to her horseback trip with a guide. Why bother with a guide? She wanted to go alone into the wilderness and learn about surviving. Her mind began to race with thoughts of what she would need and time to prepare for such a journey. The horses on the track and all the people had faded into the distance. Her mind was elsewhere in the early planning stages, being miles away.

Jeremy was looking concerned. She must endure the rest of this day with him. Soon, they walked outside to the crowded area around the track. Here, near the railing, Loren found the drive to be on a horse stronger.

Jeremy was gently asking her about betting again on her favorite. She couldn't concentrate. Finally she told him she had to go.

On the drive home, she was silent. Jeremy was curious as to what had happened to make her get into this mood. Being the gentleman that he was, he remained silent, too.

He dropped her off at her front walkway, said goodbye and left.

Almost the instant Loren entered her bedroom, she began pulling out clothes to wear on the trip she was formulating in her mind. She would take two weeks. Ride one week and then turn around and come back the same way. That way she would be familiar with the campsites and the terrain. She sat down at her desk and began to make a list. Each day was a menu of food that would travel. Apples, bananas, granola bars along with canned goods with flip tops for easy opening. As far as cooking, she would have to consult someone about the minimum things she would need. When she checked her schedule, she noted that the next two weeks were clear of any social events that needed to be attended.

A list was made of items to buy, such as a sleeping bag, small tent, flashlights, lantern and bug spray. Horses! She would need a good riding horse and probably another one to carry all the supplies. A book on how to survive the outdoors was a much needed item. Tomorrow she would set out and begin to gather her things. Hopefully the library would have a map of the area she could copy. Her excitement grew. It was stronger than it was at the horse track. If she was a believer, she would think that God had all this planned out for her.

# CHAPTER 3

Loren stood beside the horse at the stables and studied the straps and gear on the horse's saddle. The instructor was there beside her explaining everything and showing her how to tighten the saddle to keep it from slipping. Loren was thankful the horse was gentle enough and had enough patience to let her practice. Once she had it down, pat, she unsaddled the horse and repeated the whole process on her own. As she was tightening the cinch, one of her nails broke. "Ouch" They were too long anyhow. If she lost any more, she would cut them shorter. She rubbed a finger across the broken nail. With her mind back on the job at hand, she decided to test her work and swing into the saddle. It didn't slip and was on straight. She smiled in pleasure. Now, to purchase the book on how to survive in the wilderness and buy the necessary food and pack it on a second horse.

At a small stable, a little bow-legged man stood in front of his barn talking to Loren about the two horses and gear she had just rented. They were bred for mountain climbing. Both were part quarter horse. They were muscular and not as tall as the horses she had been used to riding. Ranger, was a reddish brown with a white blaze down his forehead. Two stocking feet on the front legs made him a handsome animal.

Brownie was the packhorse. He was a dark brown with a shaggy coat and sturdy short stocky legs. Both horses were well trained for their jobs. The man was wondering why she wanted to do this trip on her own. She looked like a greenhorn. He could tell she was determined to go. Maybe she would get scared and turn back. He decided to tell her about the horses and help her with the gear she would be buying.

"Now Ranger here has been taught to stand when the reins are dropped on the ground and stand still while mounting. The other horse, Brownie, has been a packhorse for a long time and will behave. When you stop for the night, run a long rope between two trees and tie a long rope to their halters. Here, I'll show you."

He showed her what to do and let her practice a couple of times. He gave her the ropes and halters with the horses.

"When do you want to pick them up?"

"I'll need to buy food for them and me for about four days. Let's say we start from here on Sunday. That will give me four days to get everything. I'll need a map of the area, too." Loren looked at the old wooden cross over the barn door. "May I ask you a question? What is the cross over your barn door?"

"Well, Missy, it signifies that I am a Christian and everyone who comes here will get a square deal. You don't know what the cross is?"

Loren shook her head. "Is it found in the Bible?"

"Yes, it is. God's Son Jesus was crucified on a cross. He died for our sins, the sins of the whole world. Most of the churches preach about that on Sundays. The thing is, we are all sinners and come short of the glory of God. He came to this world to give us eternal life and die for our sins on the cross."

"But why would they kill the Son of God? Didn't the people know who He was?"

"No, they did not know. All the high officials during that time didn't want Him around. They found reasons to falsely accuse Him so He would be put to death. Do you go to Church, Missy?"

"They are all so big and boring. The pastor speaks in monotones and puts half of us asleep. All they talk about is what a good job we are doing in the community helping the poor, etc. My mother leads a garden club that helps fund missionaries. We even gather up our old clothes and have a rummage sale. The money goes to feed the poor during the holidays."

"Then you don't consider yourself a sinner?"

"If God said it, I guess I do. I don't know what to do about it."

"Let me get something for you. Wait here."

The man limped into the office beside the barn. When he came back, he carried a worn black leather book. He handed it to her. "Take this on your trip and read the passages inside. This is God's Word and it will tell you everything you need to know about Him and Jesus, His Son."

Loren held the Bible in her hands. It was well worn and in need of good care.

"Thank you. I will read it every night. Anything else you need to tell me about the horses or the trip?"

"You'll have great weather. Supposed to be a short cold front coming through the first of the week. Pack warm clothes. It will get cold in the mountains at night. Make sure you have plenty of matches or a lighter."

Loren thanked him and left to get her food for the trip. She had really never been grocery shopping before and it was all new and turned out to be frustrating. She searched for things she could make over an open fire and open can tops. Apples and carrots along with cookies and granola bars were good snack foods.

Her clothing was chosen and a warm sleeping bag purchased along with several cooking utensils. A small pup tent that was easy to put up was purchased. Cold packs were bought and stored in the freezer to keep food cold for a couple of days.

She would then resort to canned food and the dehydrated foods that took water to activate them. A couple of pans and a skillet along with the utensils for eating and cooking were added to the list.

Sunday began as a beautiful day. Loren was on the road to the stable before eight o'clock. The man had her horses outside tied to the hitching post. He had a packsaddle on the pack horse. Loren lugged all her gear over to the horses and watched carefully while he packed her belongings on the horse. Behind the saddle of her riding horse, she had a raincoat rolled and tied in place.

Saddlebags were there, too holding her precious book on how to survive. She put the Bible that the man had given to her into her bags. Some cosmetics were in there with soap for washing and cleaning the dishes.

Loren parked her car, secured her sunglasses, a hat and her cell phone before locking the doors. She gave the man a copy of her planned trip in case she didn't return as scheduled. Walking with a spring in her step, she approached her horse. It turned its head around to look at her, then shook it. Loren laughed.

"Okay, Ranger. We'll get along just fine. You'll see." Loren fastened the loop on lead rope to the packhorse over the saddle horn of her horse. Walking back around to the left side, she easily mounted Ranger. Gathering up the reins, she turned the horse. With a short wave to the man, she started off down the road.

Her map would tell her where there would be a good place to stop for the night. The first part of the journey was on a smooth straight road. Loren was busy looking around enjoying the scenery. When a person drove a car, they couldn't look around very much at the scenery or what might be going on in the woods that surrounded them. This was a real treat. Loren could smell the pine trees that lined the road. The road was covered with the pine tree needles. The clip clop of the horse's hooves could only be heard when they hit a spot on the trail minus of the needles. Several birds sang from the treetops and a squirrel chattered nearby in its tree.

Loren watched the sun start to go down and knew it was time to get ready to make her first campsite. She searched the side of the road looking for the campground the man had spoken of. Almost automatically Ranger turned to the right on another well worn trail that was wide enough for a vehicle.

Just a little ways in Loren saw what looked like a place to camp. An old picnic table sat there along with a grill. Pieces of pine cones were scattered on the table.

The squirrels were getting ready for winter. She rode up to the table and dismounted. Her legs almost gave out on her. Boy, was she stiff! Slowly she walked around the table leading the horses. She pulled off the long rope to use as the rope between the two trees. Fastening Ranger's reins onto a bush, she set about fixing the rope. When that was done, she fastened Brownie to the rope. Glancing around the area, she spotted the small building with the restroom sign overhead. She walked over and found the outside water spigot. A bucket was there and she filled it with water. Lugging it over to a tree, she set it down. The horses were anxious for the water and kept shoving their heads toward the bucket, but she made them wait until she had them unsaddled. The halter for Ranger was pulled off the backpack and fastened around his neck until she removed the bridle. With him tied on a long rope to the tree rope, she let him get the water. The packhorse was unpacked and allowed to drink the second bucket she drew for it. She read that the animals were to be taken care of first, so she fed them their portion of grain and let them graze on the grass around them. She then went in search of a 'soft' place to pitch her tent.

The book told about pine needles making a soft bed, so she scraped up enough to put under the tent.

Loren hummed to herself as she worked setting up her first campsite. She found some charcoal where the last camper had left in the grill. Cleaning the grill off, she got her meal ready from her compact cooler. Ranger watched her in between bites of grass.

She had her survival book opened and was consulting the 'authorities' on the proper way to set up a camp. Awhile later found her on her knees trying to get the tent stakes fastened onto the tent canvas. After several attempts, she began to laugh. She could just see herself on *America's Funniest Videos* show. Her neck reddened. What if it were? Her so-called friends would get a good belly laugh from it, too. She checked the tent instructions again, finding her mistake. Grasping the correct pole, she set it where it needed to be. Everything fell into place. Folding back the tent flap, she unrolled the sleeping bag and put a few of her belongings into the tent. Ranger watched, sort of wishing he was human so he could laugh at her. She had been gentle with him in their first day on the road. He grabbed another mouthful of the tall grass near the tree where they were tied. As he chewed, he saw her holding the book as she was figuring out how to cook on the grill near the table.

Soon, the wonderful aroma of hamburger and onions on the grill assailed Loren's nose. She opened a small can of pork and beans and grabbed a cool drink. She was almost ready as she got a plate and her silverware.

She sat on the side of the table where she could watch the sun setting in the West. Beautiful! A bright orange sun lowered into the line of trees turning the clouds nearby pink and later purple. Loren put wood into the fire circle. Soon, orange flames licked around the wood and a cheery fire was started.

Later that evening, Ranger saw her pull out an apple. His mouth drooled. Maybe if he nickered softly she might offer him and Brownie a piece.

Loren was startled by his nicker. She looked at the apple and back at him. Maybe he wanted a piece. She took her knife and cut off a couple pieces and walked to him. Putting a piece on the flat of her hand, she offered him one. She did the same for Brownie.

"I have some carrot horse treats in the saddlebags, but this will do for now. I think I will try out my tent. We have another day ahead of us tomorrow."

On stiff legs, she crawled into the tent and zipped down the flap. The first day was complete. Hopefully she would sleep well this first night on the ground.

The next morning, as the sun began to peek over the hills in the distance, Loren crawled out of her tent. The minute she stood up, every muscle in her body screamed. Slowly she began to flex her muscles like she did before starting her exercise work-out at home. Soon, they loosened up enough to move about.

After her restroom trip, she opened her pack to get something out to eat that was fast and filling. The horses were given some grain and another bucket of water apiece.

Loren looked at the stack of camping gear that was supposed to go back on the packhorse. Shaking her head, she wondered how in the world the man had packed everything so tight and neat. Thankfully she remembered the order of everything. Grunting with the weight of the tent bag, she pushed it upon the packsaddle. The tent bag went up, only to slide across the pack saddle and go down onto the ground on the other side. Ranger looked at her, then gave her his best horse laugh. This was getting good! At least the lady knew how to saddle properly. She looked over at him as he had 'laughed', then hid her chuckle back. At least the horse had a sense of humor.

He was standing still and ready to go. Walking around the packhorse, she retrieved the tent bag and tried again to put it onto the packsaddle. This time it stayed put. Quickly she lashed it down with the rope and moved on to the next item.

Every other item was set on top and tied down. It was really not as neat as the man had done it, but it would stay put. Moving over to Ranger, she checked the tightness of the saddle finding it a little loose. As she was tightening it up, one of her long manicured nails broke. This was number two. No more. That was it! She looked at it as she said a few words to herself. They were really too long for this rugged way of life. Sitting down at the picnic table, she got out her manicure kit and proceeded to cut all of her nails short. With a nod of satisfaction, she looked up to see Ranger watching her. Grinning at him, she walked over and rubbed his nose.

"Good boy. Good thing you can't tell me what I am doing wrong. I don't need someone to do it. We'll get along fine. Let's get everything ready to move out."

She checked the camping area to make sure it was clean and she didn't leave anything behind. A fast trip to the restroom and they were off. She had checked the map before leaving so she knew which way to go.

The terrain was getting steeper. Large rock formations loomed on both sides of the road now, as the trail that she rode narrowed. Ranger moved slowly and carefully around a large crop of rocks. Small stones bounced across the trail as the horse's feet hit them. She guided the horses around pot holes and larger rocks that had fallen onto the trail from the rock formations above.

The edge of a cliff was now before them, down below laid a small wild valley where humans had only crossed and kept on going. The valley was full of bears and other wild animals that men had avoided over the years. The man at the stable had suggested to Loren that she ride around the valley along the cliff's edge. Even though Loren was not normally scared of heights, the trail was beginning to look scary. Loren let out the lead on Brownie some so he could follow easier. She patted Ranger's neck speaking words of encouragement to him as he picked along the dangerous trail. Even in places that there didn't seem to be a trail, Ranger found passage.

Loren promised him a whole apple when they camped for the night. She watched the slim trail seemingly leading nowhere. She couldn't see if she was going in the right direction, but there was no other trail in sight. Ranger was doing his best. She wasn't pushing him and he appreciated it. A loose rein and a pat once in awhile on the neck kept him going. Eagles winged across the open sky screeching. Far below in the mysterious valley was their prey. As Loren watched, an eagle suddenly dived down to the valley floor, hooking a small animal with its mighty talons. Swiftly it carried its prey up into the air and off to a far away tree.

A tree posed a problem. Loren was not paying attention to where she was going as she watched a hawk soaring overhead heading down to where the eagle had gotten its meal, then disappeared in the wild brush of the valley floor. Brownie went on one side of the tree and her and Ranger the other. Brownie's line jerked them to a stop. She turned to look at him looking at her from the other side of the tree.

Chuckling, she spoke.

"What are you doing over there? You silly horse. Did you miss seeing the tree? Oops, I think I should have been paying attention to where we were going. That eagle was so beautiful up there. I had never seen one before in the wild. Sorry, there, Brownie. How about a snack?"

Loren dismounted and stretched her legs. She reached into her saddlebags and pulled out the carrot treats. Offering one to both horses, she listened to them chew. Overhead the same eagle soared across the open sky screeching as it flew.

Mountains were getting higher and she was getting anxious to get to her next campsite. As she stood there, she checked over the map. Where she was, was not really on the map. Now what? Tracing her finger along the trail on the map, she tried to figure out just where she was. There was no one to ask. She whipped out her cell phone.

When she turned it on, it showed no service. Great! What good is a cell phone if you can't use it in case of an emergency!

Looking around, she couldn't see any trail that was safe to continue on. She would have to back track. A shiver coursed up her back. She was getting scared. She needed help, but there was no one around. She put the cell phone back in the saddlebags. Maybe someday someone would invent a cell phone that could be used in vast open country void of people. Brownie and Ranger were waiting quietly for their new marching orders.

# CHAPTER 4

She walked the horses down the trail that she could see. Small rocks slid out from under her feet as she maneuvered around the rocks. The trail was going down instead of up and around! Oh, oh. Now what? She had been told to stay out of the valley. Now she was heading right into it. Maybe there was a side trail. It was starting to get dark. Riding or walking in this area would be dangerous. Maybe if she camped near the edge of the valley… No, she would mount and maybe the horse can find·the trail up and out.

Dead ends was all that was available. Several appeared to go further, but had no place to camp. Somewhat dreading camping in the valley, she decided to ride down into the valley. As she rode away from the rocks she saw a small stream with water for her and the horses, plus, there were trees to which she could tie the horses.

Loren began setting up camp. She decided to leave the tent on the packhorse saddle. She was able to get it off his back though. Leaving it packed, she decided to just roll out the sleeping bag and sleep in the open. She made a large campfire ring and had a roaring fire in no time. The horses seemed content in the tall grass after being watered at the stream. Loren got out her flashlight and searched the map. This particular valley was barely on the map. A trail up and around was several miles back.

She would have to backtrack several hours to find it. She was lost!

Digging into her saddlebags, she found the Bible she had brought with her. Maybe she could get some comfort from reading God's Word. Leafing through the pages, she came upon the Psalms. She remembered someone mentioning the 23rd Psalm. Leafing through the Psalms, she found it.

*'The Lord is my shepherd; I shall not want. He maketh me to lie down in green pastures, he leadeth me beside the still waters. He restoreth my soul; he leadeth me in the paths of righteousness for his name's sake. Yea though I walk through the valley of the shadow of death, I will fear no evil; for thou are with me; thy rod and thy staff they comfort me. Thou prepares a*

*table before me in the presence of mine enemies; thou anointest my head with oil; my cup runeth over. Surely goodness and mercy shall follow me all the days of my life and I shall dwell in the house of the Lord for ever.'*

Tears formed in her eyes. God was up there watching over everyone. Was He watching out for her? The Psalms she had read gave her comfort. She was in a valley of possible death. The preacher had mentioned prayer. He called it talking to God. It was worth a try. She could really use some help here. She bowed her head and began talking to God.

"God, I know really nothing about you, but I would really like to. I am lost in a valley full of bad things and animals. I took this little journey to maybe find myself. Please watch over me and my animals. Help me get through this adventure of mine and I will try to find out how to get close to you. The young man told me You could give me peace and comfort. I could sure use some now. Amen."

She slid down into her sleeping bag and went into a peaceful sleep. During the night, a saddled horse ventured into the camp. There was fear in the horse's eyes. It had come a long way from the spot where it had lost its rider. It was glad for some of it's own company on this dark scary night.

Bright sunlight woke Loren up the next morning. She got scared when she spotted extra legs out by the horses. Slowly she climbed out of her bag and got to her feet. It was a horse! And it was saddled. Where was its rider? She walked over to the picket line and talked to the horse. The corners of its mouth was cut and bleeding where its rider had pulled on the reins too tightly. She put Ranger's bridle on and put his halter on the strange horse. Easily she removed the bridle. Taking water from the stream, she gently washed the cuts around its mouth.

She unsaddled the horse and put it on the picket line with Brownie. Saddling up Ranger, she rode down into the valley to see if she could find the rider. Deer jumped across the trail disappearing into the tall brush. Other small animals scurried about looking for food. Suddenly Ranger jerked to a halt.

He snorted and began prancing around. There on the ground ahead of them laid a still form. Loren dismounted and dropped the reins to 'ground tie' Ranger.

"Hello! Hello there." No answer. She bent down and touched him. He was still warm, but unconscious. Slowly she rolled him over. The young man was rugged looking with a beard and moustache. His dark brown hair was long and curling around his ears. A lock of it had fallen down on his forehead. Loren reached down and brushed it back.

His hat was beside him looking like it had been stomped on and dragged through the dirt. His clothes were fairly clean, just dusty from probably hitting the dirt when he was thrown off his horse. The flannel shirt he wore was tucked into a slim waistline. In all appearances, he looked like a rancher. There were spurs on his boots. She grinned. Where was his trusty six gun? Yee Haw! We have a cowboy down. He has bitten the dust! Crouching down, Loren felt his arms and legs to see if any was broken. Everything seemed okay. There was a little blood on the side of his head that might explain his being unconscious. She shook his shoulder and called out again. She was rewarded with a moan. Long dark eyelashes blinked as he opened his dark blue eyes. Loren gave him her best smile.

"Hello, there."

"Are you an angel?" He rasped. His throat was dry. Did she have some water?

Loren laughed. "Hardly. I'm just beginning to know God. What happened to you."

"My stupid horse threw me and ran away. I think it saw a snake." He saw her visibly jump in fright. Inwardly he grinned. A real lady. What was she doing out here in the wilds of the mountains and in the forbidden valley?

"What are you doing out here?"

"Right now? Evidently saving your life. Can you sit up?"

"Of course." He started to sit up. Dizziness hit him and he plopped back down.

"I thought I could. Give me a minute. Are you just riding around alone?"

"I'm alone, but not just riding. I got lost. I was riding the ridge cliff trail and I made a wrong turn several miles back. I thought the valley might be a good place to camp for the night."

The man sat up suddenly speaking loudly. "Lady, this is a dangerous valley. Where in the world are you from that you didn't know that?"

"I did know about the dangers of the valley, but I had nowhere to go. I was what you would call stuck between a rock and a hard place; literally. Okay, let's get you back to my camp. We can eat and then decide how to get out of here."

"Sounds like a plan. Name's Andy, by the way."

"I'm Loren. Can you walk or would you rather ride?"

Andy put an arm around Loren's shoulder once he got to his feet.

He was still somewhat dizzy, but he was not going to admit that to a woman. He walked along beside her with Ranger following them. When Andy felt the wave of dizziness vanish, he asked to ride.

Back at camp, Loren bathed Andy's head wound. He was impressed on her camping skills. "How long have you been camping out?"

"Actually this is my second night out. I have a book on surviving the wilderness. It is rather good. I have learned a lot. I'm actually in chapter three."

Andy let that comment go. He wasn't about to criticize her camping skills when he needed her attention. "You have a couple good horses. Did you pack yourself?"

Loren laughed. "Not when I first started out. I have a lot of ends sticking out, but everything fits. Did you get enough to eat?"

"Yes. Where are you going now?"

Loren showed Andy the map. "I was going to be out five days and then turn around and go back. Not sure what to, but people will be looking for me if I don't. Where did you come from? Is there a way out of this valley?"

"Sure. There are lots of ways out, but not from this side. My cabin is over there overlooking the valley from that mountain ridge. Why don't you bring all your gear up there and we can work out a safer passage for you."

"Okay." She watched him stride over to his horse on the picket line. He patted it on the neck, then began to tighten the saddle. He replaced the bridle. Ranger watched them as he stood on his ground tie. Loren began breaking camp. Andy helped her repack the packhorse properly and made sure the ground fire was out. Together they rode out back across the valley floor.

The sun was just coming over the peaks giving bright light to the dark valley.

"This reminds me of the 23rd Psalm I read last night. Going through the valley and fearing no evil."

Andy looked over at her. "Oh, are you a Bible scholar?"

Loren laughed. "No. I am just learning about God and His Word. I promised Him I would learn more and try to live right."

Andy snorted. 'Bible reading, my foot!' He said to himself. That was one of the reasons he had moved out into the country; to get away from Christians.

They always talked about Jesus and what He could do for them. He hadn't helped him when he needed help from the car accident that killed his fiancée. It had left him devastated. People seemed to be sympatric of his needs, but none really stayed with him to mentor him through the hard times. He had needed help, being a new Christian himself. So he retreated to this hideaway in the mountains. He had put all his energies into building the cabin and stocking it so he wouldn't have to venture out to town where people would whisper and maybe criticize his new life style. His head ached from the fall. Each bounce of the horse sent a shooting pain through his head. He had successfully hidden from all his friends and neighbors for almost two years.

From the cabin he could mope about with his memories without outside criticism. This woman was a tenderfoot. She had no business riding around in this country alone. Sneaking a peek out of the corner of his eye, he watched Loren. Even though she had been camping only two times out, she still resembled a greenhorn. He would even bet that if she saw a spider or snake, she would be heading the opposite direction.

He took the lead up the well worn trail toward his cabin. It had taken him two summers to build, but it was strong and home.

Loren watched Andy's back as he climbed the mountain trail. She could see the muscles in his broad shoulders flexing as he relaxed in the saddle. His horse was no longer scared. It climbed like it knew the trail well. Ranger had no trouble keeping up. He enjoyed a good climb, too. Brownie plodded along behind hoping to rest soon.

On top of the cliff, an area of flat land stretched out before them. A small log cabin with a couple out buildings stood in the middle. A corral was there holding a cow and another horse. The horse nickered a greeting as they came over and dismounted.

"I don't have indoor plumbing, so if you need to go to the restroom, it's that small building over there. I'll take care of your horses."

"Thank you." she replied as she began walking toward the small building that she had read about being an outhouse. Another building was open ceiling. A water tower was up behind it. She wondered if this was his shower. Peeking in the door, she confirmed the shower. She shivered thinking that only cold showers would be available. She moved on toward the outhouse. She had heard that they smelled terrible, but as she opened the door of this one, it smelled clean. It's door squeaked on its hinges as she opened it far enough to go inside. The luxury of toilet paper was there. Grinning, she wondered what other surprises she was in store for up at the house.

When Loren entered the cabin, Andy had her map spread out on the kitchen table. He was studying it closely. He glanced up as she entered. Loren took in the rustic walls of the cabin and the huge stone fireplace. Brightly colored throw blankets covered the couch and one chair. It felt at home. She walked over to the table where he was standing with her map.

"This map is fairly old and not up to date. That is probably why you missed your turn back on the cliff trail. Even that first camp ground where you stayed is really not on this map."

"My horse found the road right to it. I would have ridden right past the road even though it was a wide trail and wide enough for a vehicle. I noticed when I looked at the map the other night, that the valley is barely on the map."

"People don't come near it except during hunting season. Then they venture down and kill a couple of deer, then leave. There are bears big enough to eat you alive if you run into one on the prowl. That rattler my horse almost stepped on would have scared you up a tree."

Loren laughed. "I can't climb trees."

"You would have learned in a hurry. Your campfire was what brought me down this morning. I wanted to see what was down there."

"I'm glad you did. Now, show me on the map where I need to go to get out. I still want to get there before turning around." she said pointing at a small town about sixty miles away. She had only been traveling two days, this making the third day, but she wasn't going anywhere right then. She wanted to ride for five days, then turn around and go back.

Andy took a pen and drew a few lines for a route to take. He would ride with her to the other side of the valley where she was supposed to exit the cliff trail.

From there, she could safely make it the rest of the way with no problem.

Together they went back outside and he repacked her packhorse. She watched closely so she could do it that next morning. She wouldn't get very far that day, but at least she wouldn't be lost and she had a companion to talk to on the way, or at least a little while.

Andy went about getting something for them to eat lunch. She helped put plates and silverware on the table. Cold roast beef sandwiches and equally cold iced tea was set before her. She bowed her head to say grace. Andy watched, but didn't bow his head. They ate in silence and then cleaned up the items before going back outside. Loren checked her saddle cinch, then Brownie's. Andy got his horse's saddle tightened and mounted. Loren followed him out back behind the cabin to a well worn road leading off into the West. There, the trail was wide enough for them to ride side by side.

They rode in compatible silence for a short while, both lost in their own thoughts. Andy was curious about Loren and why she bothered to pray over her food. He knew everyone should thank God for their food, but not little rich girls. That was who she said she was when they had first met at her campsite in the valley. Was she really that much different after only a couple of days on the trail? He frowned. Maybe she was trying to change her life like she said. He had seen the worn Bible in her pack when she had it out at the campsite. Surely someone had given it to her. Clearing his throat, he ventured into putting a foot into his mouth.

"Loren, how do you really know God is with you on this trip?"

Loren looked surprised at the question. Her being a new believer, she chose her words carefully. "Andy, I have only started believing in God. I had always knew He existed, but not the part about His Son dying on a cross for our sins.

That about blew me away. You see, when I was shopping one day in town, a stranger approached me on the street. He told me about God loving me and that I could find peace if I believed in Jesus. Through the next several days, I couldn't shake the thoughts. An acquaintance of mine took me to the racetrack to watch horses race. In the Ladies Lounge, I found a Bible on the table. Inside there was a picture of Jesus standing on the side of a mountain range holding a little white lamb in His arms. I looked up the Bible passage in Matthew telling me about the lamb. If He cared that much for one little lamb, then how much do you think He cares for one of us? Then when I went to get the horses at the stable, Joel, the owner, told me about Jesus dying on the cross. He had a cross over the barn door. That was all it took for me. He gave me this Bible. I now read my Bible every day before going to bed. He has been right there beside me watching over me and the horses. No harm has come to any of us. The road to salvation seems so simple. It's the living it that is the hard part. Do you know..."

Andy cut her off. "NO! I'm not interested in God. Here's your turn." He cut his horse sharply to the left. Using a little more pressure on the bit than he really wanted to, his horse tossed its head in protest. It wasn't used to being treated roughly. Inwardly he tried hard to hold in his anger. This was a stranger. She didn't know him or what his hang-ups were. Slowly to himself, he counted to ten and breathed in slowly.

Loren lowered her head. What should she say to that? Something had hurt him and he wasn't about to tell a perfect stranger. She would keep praying for him and keep her faith strong. As she watched where they were going, the trail opened out of the forest onto an open road leading down into another valley. From there would be a short two day journey to Waverly.

# CHAPTER 5

Another eagle winged across the sky over the valley. Several other small birds were taking wing to search for food. The scenery was breathtaking! So many colors in the rocks and the shades of the brush at their edge.

Loren decided to change the subject. “It is so peaceful here, Andy. I can see why you would like the solitude here. Do you get to town very often?”

Andy let his anger simmer and was thankful she had changed the subject. “Just for supplies. I have a four wheel drive jeep in one of the sheds that I drive down twice a month. Not much grain or grass up here for the animals. Sometimes I take them down in the valley when I feel that it is safe.

“What about loneliness? Don’t you get lonely?”

Andy looked at her, then around at the scenery about them. Sure he got lonely.

Maybe he should get a dog. He rubbed a hand across the small bump on his head where he had fallen. Women were handy to have around once in awhile. This one with him now could prove very interesting outside her element. Where was she from anyhow?

"Say, Loren, where are you from? What made you decide to come out here especially on a horse?"

Loren chuckled. "Andy, I told you that I am a spoiled rich girl who doesn't do anything except what I want to do and what my curiosity gets me into. My latest interest is horseback riding. When I went to the racetrack and I watched all those wonderful creatures running, I just had to try it. Although, I haven't really tried to gallop Ranger, we seem to be doing fine at a walk."

Loren looked around once more at the beautiful scenery. Andy's attitude had changed and she didn't want to upset him any further. Even though she wanted to stay longer, Ranger was pulling on the reins, he wanted to go.

"Wal, little rich girl, here is where I can leave you." drawled Andy in his best cowboy impersonation. "You'all come back and see me."

"Oh, do cell phones work out here?"

"No, thank goodness. Were you going to call me?"

"Yes, when I come close to this spot on my way back. Maybe we can meet somewhere for a cup of coffee down there. I can almost see a town from here."

"Sure." He watched her. He wanted to get to know her better. He was almost reluctant to say goodbye. Reluctantly he turned his horse back around.

Even this brief time with Andy, Loren had wanted it to last longer.

She watched him as he turned his horse around and started back down the trail.

"Andy? Maybe when I get back this way in a couple of days we can run the horses across the valley? It sounds like it would be invigorating to have the wind blow across your face at a fast pace."

Andy turned the horse around and grinned. "You'd better believe it. There's almost nothing like it. See you in, what? Three or four days?"

"I think so. Can we meet right here?"

"Yes. See you then. Bye Loren."

She listened to the clip clop of his horse's hooves as they began to pick up speed and watched him lope the horse back down the trail. Already she missed his closeness; an experience she had never had before. Could God be changing her way of thinking about men? Grinning to herself, she nudged Ranger ahead. She hoped so. She desperately needed to change her life.

That had been the whole reason for this trip alone in the elements. Ranger drew her attention back to the present when he reached for a long stem of grass along the road. The reins were pulled loose and she sat up straighter.

"All right, horse. Didn't I give you a nice treat before we left Andy's? You are still hungry? Well, you *do* eat like a horse." She laughed out loud. It felt good to laugh as well as feel the sun on her bare arms. With one hand, she tugged her hat on tighter. With another nudge in Ranger's side, he gave a snort and began to trot.

Bouncing about in the saddle caused her to grab the horn and pull back on the reins.

"Easy Ranger. I didn't realize the next speed would be so rough."

She patted his neck and let him settle back into a fast walk instead.

The scenery began to change once more. The mountains opened out into another larger valley where the landscape was spotted with farms. Vehicle traffic was sparse, but present. While nice neat little homes lined the road that she traveled.

People watched her ride by on her way past civilization and on toward the countryside once more. Her supplies were in good shape and she didn't need anything from the store in the small town. Andy told her about a larger town at the end of her journey, yet sixty miles ahead. There she would stock up on everything and turn back.

At the other side of the small town, she stopped to look at the map and let the horses drink from the water trough near the windmill. She found a restroom and spent a few minutes in there. When she came back out, she got an apple from the saddlebags and cut it up. She gave some to both horses and ate the other half. Loren checked the tightness of Ranger's saddle and the packhorse, then remounted. Glancing at her watch, she figured she had just enough time to reach the KOA before dark.

Several campers watched her set up camp on her spot near the back of the park.

This time, she had a small corral where the horses could walk about free without being tied. Several of the young children camping there came by to pet the horses. Loren let a couple of the older ones brush the horses. She put their grain in the collapsible buckets and hung them on the fence. Ranger nickered at her as she walked by. She laid her head against his cheek and rubbed his neck. Such a good horse. Brownie was busy on the bale of hay at the far side of the corral was too busy to pay any attention to her or his traveling buddy.

Brownie was glad to be free of the rope and backpack. After a good roll in the dirt, he was ready to eat some more. The nice clean brushing was long gone.

Brownie liked being dusty. Ranger tossed his head and pranced around the corral. He even threw in a couple of bucks getting rid of his pent up energy. He wished she had ridden him a little faster so he would be really tired at the end of their day. Maybe he could challenge that man's horse to a race if they went back to his cabin. With a snort, he stopped in the middle of the corral and whirled around. Shaking off the dust, he was now content to eat the hay offered to them in the corral.

Loren came back from the campground store with a couple of hot dogs and buns. She already had a can of beans to eat with them. A small fire was started and she whittled a point on a stick that she had found laying nearby. This was so much fun! The thoughts of Jeremy crossed her mind. The conceited man wouldn't have lasted a day, let alone a week. She was going for two weeks. Her saddle soreness had long ago ceased. Easily she moved about the campsite enjoying the time outdoors.

With her tent up and everything ready for bed, she took a couple of carrot treats to the horses. They eagerly took them, chewing slowly to savor the flavor.

She found a chair under a light and sat down. She opened her Bible and began to read more of Psalms. It was a comforting time before she turned in for the night. Andy's response to her testimony was disturbing. She said a special prayer for him at the close of her Bible reading. Closing her eyes, she sat there alone in the dark. Listening to the shuffling of the horses' feet in the corral along with the voices of the other campers nearby relaxed her. Soon, she was sleepy and ready to crawl into her sleeping bag.

Yawning, she got up and went into her tent. She had another day was ahead of her.

The next morning before riding out, Loren checked at the office for a weather report. A thunderstorm was predicted later that day. The man suggested she find shelter early. He gave her another map to have for the area beyond where they were now.

Another KOA was at the end of her journey, but she wouldn't make it that night.

It was around lunchtime that Loren noticed the clouds building up. They were turning black and the winds were picking up speed. Leaves were flying from the trees nearby. Several birds flew past seeking shelter. She began looking around for somewhere to go. An old abandoned barn was off to the right of the road. She reined Ranger toward it. Lightening streaked across the sky. Brownie neighed jerking on the rope. She urged Ranger faster and he walked his fastest without getting into the rough trot. She swung off in front of the barn door and dropped his reins. The large heavy wood door was stubborn. She pulled with all her strength and finally got it to open.

It protested on creaky hinges and the wind caused it to bang back against the wall tearing it from her grasp. Ranger and Brownie needed no encouragement to enter the dark barn. Musty smells assailed their noses, but the thoughts of shelter from a bad forming storm ruled over the unpleasant smells. Loren went back outside and pulled the big door closed. The wood bar was put down to keep it closed. She then unsaddled the horses. There were a couple empty stalls and she put them each in one of their own. The hay on the floor seemed somewhat fresh. They could eat that along with the grain. With a large clap of thunder, the barn walls seemed to shake. Both horses shivered in fear.

Even though they were safely inside, they were still scared. Loren talked low soothing tones to them. She ran her hands over their necks in an attempt to calm them down. Lightening flashed. She was scared of lightening, too. The patter of rain falling could now be heard on the roof. As the seconds went by, rain began to fall slowly at first then in torrents.

The rain was coming in the broken barn windows in the barn but it didn't bother the horses or Loren. With each clap of thunder, their heads shot up from eating. The whites of their eyes were present in their fear of the storm. Loren had her Bible out and was reading more in Psalms. There was comfort there and in several verses King David (who wrote some of the Psalms) talked about being in storms. He found comfort in calling upon the Lord. She read those Psalms aloud to the horses. Loren laid the Bible down and clasped her hands in front of her.

Bowing her head, she prayed silently for her safety and thanked Him for getting her safely to where she was now. In an afterthought, she mentioned Andy. He needed prayer, too. She closed with 'Amen' then leaned back to listen to the rain.

The sky was dark as night and a sudden stillness came. The horses were suddenly restless. Outside, a tornado was sweeping across the area close to the old barn. The shingles on the roof began flying off leaving open areas where the rain was coming down. The noise was deafening. Unknown objects banged against the building. A large tree top came tearing into the barn through a broken window. Splinters of wood from the window frame flew through the air. The tree branches stretched out into the passageway between the stalls where Loren sat. Leaves from the tree littered the barn floor. She was safe. Her faith in God to protect them held true. She used her flashlight to look at her watch It was only one o'clock in the afternoon and dark as night.

Should she just stay there for the night? She decided to wait another hour and see. Meanwhile, she went back to her Bible and just opened it and began to read.

# CHAPTER 6

Light came through the front window and soon the sun began to shine. The storm was over. Loren lifted the bar on the barn door and shoved it open. Several large trees were down across the road. Roof shingles were scattered all over the ground. She walked around to where the tree that had come through the window had stood.

Its roots were pulled out of the ground. Fortunately no other structures nearby had been hit.

All of the storm's fury had been near the old barn. Loren shivered with the thought. God had protected them. The storm had passed by. They were safe.

She checked her watch. They had time to ride further. Looking at the map she had gotten at the KOA showed a possible campsite an hour's ride from there. She would go there and spend the night.

"Okay, Ranger, let's go fella. We can get a little further before night catches us."

Within a short time, she had both horses ready to travel. She led them out of the barn and closed the door. Glancing up in the now blue sky, she whispered a 'thank you'.

Ranger went off in his shuffling walk down the road after avoiding all the downed trees and large puddles of water. Loren saw destruction all along the way.

Several people were outside starting their clean-up process. The buzz of chain saws were beginning to fill the air. No one really paid any attention to her as she rode past. The area was soon left behind and so was the destruction. An ambulance came whizzing by with its lights and sirens blaring. Ranger snorted, but held his ground. He wasn't disturbed by loud noises. Brownie tried to pull loose in an effort to runaway. He soon calmed down after the ambulance had disappeared down the street.

When Loren spotted the new campsite, she smiled with pleasure. It was a beautiful spot! A small stream crossed through it with a weeping willow tree down near its bank. There were no tables, chairs, rocks, or even large logs to sit on at this campsite. Several pine trees stood back together on the other side. Pine needles were plentiful for bedding under her sleeping bag. Wood for a small fire was scattered about to be picked up. Tall grass waved in the gentle breeze that beckoned to the hungry horses.

Loren set up camp. She unsaddled both horses and gave them a good brushing. With the horses fed from their grain sack, she walked about gathering wood for her fire. She decided to try the dehydrated package of beef stew and the biscuits in a can.

Setting out her pan, she fashioned a rod across the fire and hung her pot full of the stew. Her ice packs were getting soft. She would need to eat all her perishables soon. Several apples were cut up and doled out to the horses and her. She opened a can of peaches for dessert.

Sitting cross-legged on the ground before the fire, she truly felt like a cowboy. Being isolated, she took the chance to remove her clothes and bathe in the stream. Cold water caused her to eeek and almost forget the thought of getting clean. In just a short time, she became accustomed to the cold water and splashed around.

It felt good to be clean from head to toe. Ranger watched, shaking his head in amazement. He was beginning to like this woman. He had forgotten all of his tricks that he usually played on his riders.

Feeling one hundred percent better, Loren put on clean clothes. Loren then took her dirty ones back down to the stream, and figured out how to wash them. She then hung the damp clothes on the extra rope where the horses were tied. Ranger stretched out his nose and sniffed at her underwear causing her to laugh and shove his face away.

"You silly horse! Don't even think about trying to chew them." she rubbed his neck and nose. A scratch or two behind his ears made him really feel good.

The sunset was beautiful. She watched it until the last of the reds and oranges faded away into the dark purple of the night sky. If this trip did nothing to her personal situation, she did get to enjoy the sunsets and scenery all around her.

Just two more days before she reached the larger town where she would buy more supplies and turn back toward home. She checked on the horses and went over to her sleeping bag and crawled in. At peace, now, she began to think about Andy. Andy could live a life in solitude like this. Could she? Being around her parents and their friends had caused her boredom. All her activities to ease that boredom had not been a permanent fix. Could this new found faith in God change all that? She was willing to give it her best shot. She felt a closeness to God out here among the creation He had made. She would talk to Andy again and see what he thought about her new found faith and situation. In the meantime, she would continue to read her Bible and grow in her knowledge of the Word of God. She stretched from her stiff sitting position and put a hand across her mouth covering a huge yawn. It had been a long day!

Sleep finally found her resting peacefully on the ground under the pine trees. Night sounds of the running water in the stream, the crickets and tree frogs sang to her. Peacefully she slept. The wild animals; raccoons and possums traveled nearby, but didn't bother her camp.

As she was saddling up Brownie, she noticed he was holding up a front leg. Slowly Loren ran her hands down his leg. The shoe was loose, and there was nothing she could do about it now. Maybe someone at one of the farmhouses that she would pass would know of someone to help her.

The trip onward was slower to help Brownie walk comfortably. A woman was at a mailbox at the first farmhouse at the edge of a small town. Loren rode over.

"Excuse me, madam. Do you know where I can get a farrier?"

The slightly built woman in a faded flowered housedress turned her face upward. A smile spread on her face. "My husband does horses. Come on in. How about a cup of coffee?"

"I would love some. Thank you."

When they came up to the house, she went inside to summon her husband. Loren dismounted and looped

Ranger's reins over a post. A huge man with thick broad shoulders and a slim waist came out of the house, followed by his wife. He had been in the process of shaving and Loren could see some of the shaving cream around the edges of his jaw. He came over to Brownie's side and lifted the leg. He went about checking his other three feet for loose shoes.

"Let me check your mount, too, madam." Ranger was checked and all was well with his feet. He walked off to a shed where he entered. A few minutes later he returned with all his tools. Brownie was led over to another post and tied for the man to work. Loren followed the wife into the house. The smell of fresh brewed coffee reached her nose. She breathed in deeply. She hadn't had any coffee since she left home.

Another wonderful smell came with the coffee from the oven. With a pair of oven mitts, the woman pulled out a pan of cinnamon rolls. Loren's mouth began to water. They looked Sooooo good!

She watched the woman slather them with icing and watched the icing drip down their sides. Using a spatula she scooped off a couple onto a plate. "Here. I know you can eat these. Let me get the coffee. George will be back in to get his later."

Loren closed her eyes as the flavor of the cinnamon roll was slowly chewed. Its icing still warm and dripping. She opened her eyes long enough to sip the delicious coffee before taking another bite. The screen door banged shut as George entered.

"All ready to go. Good thing that happened close by. There's not another farrier between here and Waverly. Where are you heading?"

"Waverly. I am going to stock up my supplies and turn around and go back home; a five day journey from here. How much do I owe you?"

George chuckled. "Just help me eat those cinnamon rolls, will you?" he patted his flat stomach. "I want to keep my girlish figure."

His wife playfully hit him on the shoulder. "Very funny, George. Eat one and drink some coffee while I get your bacon and eggs started. Oh, would you like to have breakfast with us?"

"Oh no thank you! I ate back at my campsite about an hour or so ago. Maybe I could use your restroom before I leave?"

She pointed the way for Loren and set about fixing a bag of a couple cinnamon rolls for her to take with her. It was good having some company. As Loren came back into the room, she thrust the brown bag into her hands.

"Here's a couple for the road. Would you mind very much if we had a prayer with you for your safe journey?"

Loren was deeply touched. Tears threatened to spring up behind her eyes. Blinking, she nodded, being choked up beyond words.

She felt the woman take her hand and the three stood together. George said a short prayer for her safety and then went off to wash up for breakfast. Loren went outside followed by the wife. She watched Loren check the saddle, then swing up. Ranger turned back toward the main road. Loren waved good-by. Never before had she felt so close to God. There were others out there who loved and served God. She was blessed.

She pushed Ranger into his fast pace and made good time the rest of the morning.

When she stopped for lunch, she gave both horses an apple and she sat down with a cinnamon roll and a warm canned drink. Soon she would be in Waverly. Andy had told her it was a fairly large town. Finding a place to put the horses might be a problem. The map that she had gotten from the KOA manager had shown a campground just outside Waverly. She would go there, leave the horses and camping gear, then go into town to buy the supplies. Somehow she would manage to get them back to the campgrounds. Everything was working out great. God was definitely with her. She just knew it.

# CHAPTER 7

Loren pulled Ranger up at the top of a hill overlooking the sprawling town of Waverly. All sizes of homes were neatly placed alongside well marked streets. The landscaping showed that people took good care of their homes. It was big town; it could almost be a city from where she sat. She dreaded riding through on a horse. As she watched for smaller roads that might go around, she could almost see the KOA sign off in the distance. Slowly she nudged Ranger forward.

"Okay, big guy. This is the end of our journey for we will be turning around and going back home. When I get you both settled, I will buy more apples and carrot treats for you. Doesn't that sound good?"

Ranger tossed his head, gave her a small nicker and walked on down the road toward the large town. Loren rode down several side streets to skirt the busiest part. She spotted a grocery store nearby and noted the street name. Children of all ages came out to see the strange sight of someone riding a horse past their homes. She waved to all of them and kept going. A half hour later found her at the entrance of the KOA. They had a similar set up in the back of their campgrounds with a small corral and horse stalls. Evidently other horsemen used this park. She signed into the office and then led the horses back to the corral. Being on the ground walking felt good to her stiff muscles. She held the gate open to the corral after unsaddling both horses. Ranger trotted into the corral and did his bucking and acting like a wild horse before he got down and rolled in the dirt. With a little grunt of pleasure, he stood on sprawled out legs and shook himself. Looking forward to his grain, Ranger walked around the edges of the corral while waiting for Brownie.

Brownie patiently waited his turn. He had a lot more gear on his back to come off. Loren unsnapped the lead and turned him loose. She watched as Brownie went over to the far side in search of hay or some strands of grass he could reach from under the fence. Finding none, he did his rolling about to get dusty. Loren carried all of the gear over to a campsite she had chosen nearby. She put up the tent and stored everything inside, then zipped it shut. Her containers were emptied and cleaned out in preparation to obtain more supplies. Hearing someone coming, she looked up to see the manager riding toward her in a golf cart.

"I see you are all set up already. Would you like to use this golf cart to ride to town to get your new supplies? Just drive me back to the office and you can take it."

"Thank you. I would. I found a grocery store, but not a feed store to buy my grain."

"Let me show you our little town map." He opened up a small map that he had stored in a pocket on the cart. He spread it out on the seat and Loren looked at it as he was showing her where the feed store was located. It didn't look very far from the grocery.

"No hurry on returning the cart. I won't need it until later tonight when I make my rounds of the campground. Be careful driving in town. It is safe, but there seems to be extra people in town down at the large hotel on Main Street."

With the manager safely dropped off at the office, Loren drove toward town. She decided to tour the town before getting her supplies. Actually, she wanted to wait until the following day to get her perishables. Feed for the horses was more important tonight.

A thick steak and baked potato with all the trimmings sounded super good. Maybe she could even splurge and go to the restaurant in the hotel for a nice dinner. That would mean a walk into town. The manager would need the cart and it really wasn't equipped to be driven at night in town.

As she drove down the main street, she looked at a big black Avalanche Chevy truck parked across from the hotel. On its side advertised her father's company. Was he here? She steered the cart into a parking space next to the truck. Turning off the key, she climbed out and walked toward the hotel. Looking down at her appearance, she wrinkled up her nose. She really needed to get cleaned up first. She smelled like a horse and was dusty from the long ride that day. Before she reached the front steps, she stopped. No, this was wrong and not the right time. She turned on her heel and went back to the golf cart. If her father was in there, showing up in her unclean condition would not be good. In fact, the whole trip to town was wrong right then. She drove back to the campsite and gathered up some clean clothes and hit the showers.

The next trip to town was better. She parked the golf cart near the hotel. She was at least clean but still not presentable. A dress shop near the hotel offered an alternative. She purchased a dress and things to go with the dress. She twirled around in front of the full length mirror in the dressing room. The vision before her was back to her normal appearance, one that her dad would appreciate. Her hair was almost dry and done up into a tight bun on her neck. A colorful scarf was casually wrapped around it. Now, she would enter the hotel and seek out her father.

Back in a room off from the main lobby, she spotted him along with several other men she did not know. His tall ramrod straight figure with his snow white hair made a strong impression of anyone looking at him. He possessed power and required respect.

His full moustache twitched as his blue eyes zeroed in on her. For a second, he didn't recognize her, then his expression changed to wonder. What was she doing way out here?

Loren saw the look of recognition and smiled. She loved her father and he her. They were cut from the same cloth and she was destined to take over upon his retirement. Her light blue dress had a full skirt that swung with her long easy strides to her father's side. Her sandals clicked some on the terrazzo floor.

He put an arm about her shoulder and introduced her to his companions. He noticed the tanned skin and the healthy look of her. She had been doing something outdoors. Slowly he put a hand on each of her shoulders and turned her toward him. He smiled.

"Loren, honey, you look positively ravishing. What are you doing here?"

Loren blushed. Her dad would think her foolish, but then again, maybe not.

"I have been riding horseback through the mountains and camping outside along the way. I'm camping right now at the KOA outside of town."

"Are you serious? Loren, you shouldn't do that all alone. What were you thinking? When I finish my business here, you will go home with me."

"No, dad. If we can sit together, I will tell you what is going on and why I am doing it. Dinner tonight, here?"

"Yes. I'll come out and pick you up."

"All right. The manager needs the golf cart I am using tonight. I am on Site 25 back beside the horse corral."

Loren smiled up at him, then bid him good-bye. Mr. Grayson stood alone and watched his daughter walk toward the front door of the hotel. With a half smile on his face, he slowly shook his head. His little girl was growing up. He noticed the new way she carried herself and the way she talked told him she now had a purpose in life. Tonight, he would find out what had possessed her to make this dangerous journey alone and on a horse? He didn't even know that she could ride. Maybe that was her new interest. Jeremy had taken her to the race track. That could have inspired her. One of the men he had been with called to him and his attention was back on his business.

Later that evening, Loren sat beside her father in the Avalanche on the drive back to town. It was dark and he couldn't see the horses that she had in the corral. She had fed them and then made sure her camp was secure before leaving. She watched the play of emotions across her father's face.

When she was little, she used to imagine what he was thinking at the different faces he made. Now, she could pretty well read them. A shiver went down her back as she spotted a new one she could not identify. Her hand became sweaty as she rubbed it against the soft grain of the leather seat. Maybe she should change the subject and get him to tell her what he was doing there. No, she just better level with him and stand up for herself. She glanced once more at him before the truck was parked and the engine shut off. He patted her hand and offered her a smile. That was at least encouraging. She slid down out of the high truck onto the concrete. She smiled a little to herself. He had kept his emotions quiet and to himself. His hand found the small of her back as he ushered her into the hotel. A doorman held open the door for them to enter. A waiter all dressed in black and a starched white shirt, showed them to a table back by a window.

Another waiter came along and filled the water glasses and laid a menu in front of each of them. Her father took one glance at the entrees and put the menu down. His blue piercing eyes stared at Loren. She held his look with her brown eyes. She was good at this game he always played with her. She had never lowered her glance and had won his approval. She would do it again tonight. Her Bible reading and prayer before he had picked her up would give her the courage to face anything he would toss out at her.

"Do you want to tell me now or wait until after we eat?"

"I don't want to ruin a good meal, but I would like to start at the beginning. You have known me and know what I have been going through to be happy. Dad, I have been bored out of my skull. I can't, let me change that. I couldn't find happiness in anything I did. Everything was a temporary fix. The pleasure was only for a few hours, days or weeks sometimes. Now, I feel free and alive. A couple of weeks before Jon and Gracie's wedding reception I met a young man who…"

"What happened?" her dad cut in, being the protective father that he was. She reached over and put a hand on his. He quickly noticed the broken nails that were once long and manicured. A small frown changed his facial expression.

"Easy, dad. Let me continue. He was just a man on the street corner. A young preacher. He told me about Jesus Christ and that God can give me peace and comfort. Said I should read the Bible and attend Church. Even pray for help and guidance. Well, dad, I have done that. I haven't gone to Church yet, but I have asked Jesus to come into my life and help me. I read my Bible and pray every day. You would be amazed at all the things that I have come up against and He has seen me through. My faith is getting stronger, too. I meet other people who share the same experience.

The other day, Brownie's shoe was coming off. I found a farrier at the first house I stopped at. Guess what? They prayed with me as I was preparing to leave that I would have a safe journey. God is real in my life now."

Mr. Grayson looked at his daughter. In a way she sounded like one of those religious Bible thumpers, but then again, she didn't. Maybe it was just a faze she was going through and would soon be her old self. She had said her old self was bored and restless. She would not go back to that way of life. He would continue to listen as she went on to tell her about camping out and getting lost. She even mentioned saving Andy from his fall and then he in turn helped her out of being lost in the valley. He began to realize that he really didn't know his daughter. His Company had been keeping him busy all hours of the day and sometimes on the weekends. She had been used to playing golf or going out on the boat with him when she was younger. Now, he didn't have time to do that himself. He held her hand in his and rubbed her palm. Quickly he noticed the small calluses where her hands used to be soft and smooth. He turned her hand over and looked at the calluses. He softly rubbed them, noticing again the broken nails. She had a healthy glow about her, too. He liked that. He had known how pale and listless she was getting, but really didn't know what to do about it. He had let it go and for her to find her own way. Her fairly new mother had her own interests and didn't care much for showing Loren how to become a 'real' lady. He glanced up and spotted the waiter coming back toward them.

The waiter came back for their order and then went away again. Loren looked out the window. The night sky was turning purple from the sundown. Several birds flew across her vision out the window. A smile crossed her face. So many wonderful signs of God all about her. Loren looked up at her dad. Would her dad listen and allow her to continue her ride back home? He usually allowed her anything she wanted. Even the moon, if it was possible to obtain.

"Dad, would you like to come out to the campgrounds and meet my horses in the morning? I am going to stock up on food supplies before starting back later tomorrow."

She had grown up and sounded like she had taken on some responsibility by taking care of two horses. She looked like she had muscled up and had the trim body that most young women would die for. How had she done all of this? Mr. Grayson cleared his throat.

"Would you like to work at something in the company when you get back? I'm sure we can find something that you can learn to do." He proposed, not really sure what to do about her in the future. Someday she needed to be primed to take over the Company. Hopefully she would agree and start soon. He wanted to retire and travel, but needed someone in charge that could take over and run the company smoothly.

"I might just like that, dad. Does this mean I can continue my ride?"

He smiled. "Yes, dear daughter. I see the change in you and am pleased that you have found something worth doing and sticking with it. When do you think you will be home?"

"I took five days to come and I will probably take that long going back. I know where the roads are now and won't get lost. When I reach Andy's cut off, he will help me find the right road around the cliffs. Dad, I am really getting into this. Maybe sometime you can go camping with me. I know Mom would not unless we have an RV."

Mr. Grayson laughed. "You are right there, Loren. Maybe we can go fishing like we used to do. We'll find a campsite on a lake where we can rent a boat."

He caught the eye of the waiter and gave him a slight nod. The waiter turned back to the kitchen to bring out their meal.

As the delicious looking steak and steamy baked potato sat before them, Loren asked her dad if he minded if she prayed over the meal. He shook his head and bowed his head along with her. As with the steak and baked potato, Loren savored each bite she had had with the cinnamon rolls. If only they would keep in her ice pack and not take so long to cook, she would be tempted to fix herself steak and a baked potato every night on the road.

At the close of the meal, he drove her back to the campsite. She hugged him as they stood beside the corral fence. Ranger nickered a greeting, shoving his nose against her shoulder. He hadn't forgotten the promised apple that awaited him.

Loren hugged her dad tightly. She breathed in the smell of his favorite aftershave. He bent his head to look down on her. His chin rubbed the top of her head affectionately.

"You are growing up on me, kiddo. I wish your mom understood us. We can come down from our snooty upper class friends and be ourselves. She seems to be stuck there with her high society friends and afraid to let her hair down. We must try to do something about that when you get home. Sleep well, little one. I'll come back in the morning. Are you sleeping in?"

Loren laughed. "No, dad. I will probably be up around seven. I'll feed the horses and, say, how about a breakfast over a campfire? Can you come, dad?"

He laughed as he pulled her into his arms. "Sure. Do you remember how I like my eggs?"

She nodded, her head still close to his chest. She could get enough eggs and bacon to get by for that breakfast, then go to the grocery to stock up. She watched the tail lights of his Avalanche go off toward town. Ranger nickered again. Smiling, she turned toward him and took his head into her hands. He affectionately nuzzled her.

He stopped long enough for her to go get that apple she had promised him, then came eagerly to the fence once more. Brownie was right beside him when he smelled the juice of the apple. Politely they took the apple slices from her hands. She watched as they almost closed their eyes in enjoyment of its flavor. Inwardly she chuckled.

It was like her tonight with the steak and potato. It was truly a treat. Getting her Bible from the tent, she walked over to the bench under the light post. Sitting down, she opened it and began reading. Loren was too wound up to sleep. Seeing her dad gave her mixed feelings. True, he had let her continue her trip, but only because he had always let her do what she wanted. She could tell he was pleased with her new look. She had caught the frown when he noticed her broken nails and calluses. When she returned to her old life, maybe she would let her nails grow again. Her hair desperately needed to be done. She had been wearing it in a pony tail throughout the whole trip. None of her old friends would recognize her now. They would definitely snub her. Covering up a yawn with one hand, she closed her Bible. Sighing, she walked off toward the restroom to get ready for bed.

The way back would be easier now that she was familiar with the route. A little excitement grew as she thought of Andy and the running of the horses in the valley. Could she hang onto Ranger? Surely the running pace would be smoother than the trot.

Before she turned in for the night, she talked to Ranger as he stood beside her enjoying the immensely pleasing ear scratching. Too bad she was a human. He could fall easily in love with her. Brownie allowed some scratching, but his interest was eating.

The hay left on the ground beckoned to Brownie and he walked away.

Loren climbed into her tent and slept. Parts of her night was dreaming of her past adventures and some hopeful ones to come. Morning was bright as the sun beat her up.

She went about preparing breakfast. The bacon was almost done when her father drove up. He gave her a friendly wave as he stepped out of the Avalanche. The manager of the KOA had given her a disposable table covering and paper plates. Mr. Grayson brought over a thermos of coffee from the hotel.

"Good morning, honey. I brought some coffee. Thought it would be a nice treat since you won't have any for a week." He set the thermos down on the table. Glancing around him, he saw the neat campsite and he took in a deep breath. Bacon sizzled on the grill. His Loren had learned how to cook! He sat at the picnic table and watched her break the eggs into a skillet. He reached for the coffee cups and poured each of them a cup. His hand went into his pocket and pulled out a couple of sugar envelopes along with creamers.

"Boy, this is really roughing it. How did you learn to do all of this, camping stuff?"

"I bought a book on how to survive in the outdoors. I have really learned a lot. You should have seen me that first night trying to put up the tent. I had to look at the directions! If the Home Show Funniest Videos film crew was nearby, they would have gotten some great footage." She laughed with him. "Bring over the plates, dad. The eggs are ready."

When they sat down, Loren had a short prayer. "Thank you God for all you have done for us so far. Keep us all safe today and when we get back on the trail. Thank you for the food we are about to eat and the wonderful visit from my father. Amen"

Mr. Grayson moved his fork around on his plate to get a piece of the egg. With his head down concentrating on capturing a piece, he was really hiding the tears starting to form in his eyes. He hadn't thought much about God or what He could do in a person's life. He had generally done everything his way and plowed ahead to get it done.

When Loren wasn't looking, he swiped back the tears that threatened to fall. His second marriage hadn't been the greatest, but Loren seemed to have survived all the neglect his wife had given her. Maybe she had felt that the girl was a grown up and didn't need any more help or advice. He was pleased by her present state. She seemed ready to conquer the world. Hopefully she could finish this ride of hers and be willing to join him in working with the company. He had planned to leave most of the holdings to her anyhow upon his retirement in a couple of years. Even his plans were up in the air at the present time. Maybe he should consider God coming into his life to change it for the better. The way the stock market was going and his sales, it wouldn't hurt to have Someone of higher power in charge of his life.

He took a couple more bites of the eggs and wiped the yellow around the plate with a piece of bread that had been toasted on the grill. He hadn't had a meal like this since he was in boy scouts as a youngster. He seemed to have missed a lot growing up.

They talked for awhile before he got ready to leave. Slowly they walked over to the corral where he was introduced to Ranger and Brownie. Being a lover of horses, too, he could see the intelligence in Ranger's eyes. He looked like a good dependable horse for his daughter to have under her. Slowly they walked together back toward the Avalanche. As they reached the side of his vehicle, he pulled out a wad of money. Thumbing through about half of it, he offered it to Loren.

"Here's some money for your trip. Before you threaten to refuse it, consider it your allowance."

Loren took the money, putting into her billfold. "Thanks, dad. I'll give you a call in a couple of days to let you know how I am doing. I have my cell, but it doesn't seem to work out here in the wild open spaces. I really needed it several days ago when I got lost, but I couldn't get any signal."

"I can fix that." He went to a side compartment of his truck bed. He found a phone that was so sophisticated electronically that it would carry several miles further than a cell phone. It was an experimental model still in R&D but guaranteed to work. He handed it to her. "This will work anywhere. Use it in case of an emergency. If you speed dial, my number is number one. It works on solar power so no batteries will be needed. We have been experimenting with this at work. Let me know how good it is. Just call when you get lonesome. I'll be there for you."

"Oh, dad, Thank you! You're the best!" She hugged him tightly letting her tears flow freely. She glanced up at him and saw his watery eyes looking down on her. Maybe this trip was going to really turn everything around in a good way. The manager of the KOA came along about that time in his golf cart. He waved.

"Do you want to use the cart this morning?"

Loren turned to him, smiling. "I certainly do. Thanks. This is my father. He is one of the guests at the hotel in town. I didn't know he was coming, so he surprised me."

"It must have been a good surprise. Glad to meet you, sir. Your daughter seems to be a good camper. Don't know of any other woman who would ride across country alone and camp out. I'll walk back to the office. Bring it back when you are done. See you later."

Loren watched her dad's Avalanche drive back toward town. She cleaned up the campsite and climbed into the golf cart. She had groceries to buy and to pack for the trip.

She didn't know that they had been watched.

Two men stood behind a couple of bushes. They had seen the wad of money her dad had given her. Greedily they licked their lips. That money could be their ticket out of the area and this hick town. They moved away and made plans to waylay her when she left town with the horses. There were too many people around the camping area to try anything there. Even the grocery store where she was heading would be too crowded. They followed her around the town as she shopped.

Soon everything was purchased, so Loren went back to the campsite and started to pack.

Everything would be ready for travel in the morning. One of the feed buckets sprung a leak and had to be replaced. She had a chance to use the laundromat and wash up everything. She even spent time at a beauty shop getting her hair washed and styled. Grinning to herself, she knew the style wouldn't last very long, but the woman in her let it make her feel one hundred percent better.

# CHAPTER 8

As she sat at the picnic table watching the sunset while finishing off a brownie, she called her dad on the new phone. He caught it on the second ring. The happiness in his voice made the loneliness she felt vanish.

"Guess what, honey. Your mom has agreed to go camping." Laughing, he added, "Of course in a RV that we shopped for today. Would you like to meet us somewhere near home?"

"Dad, it would have to be where I can have my horses. Check a KOA Campground catalog. I really don't know what day I would be coming home. I'll have to let you know. I am leaving this KOA in the morning."

Loren talked for a few more minutes before hanging up. Just the thought of being with her parents at the end of this trip caused her to feel depressed. Sure she loved her parents, but it was not the ending of a trip she wanted. Turning to her Bible, she wiggled around to get comfortable, then read. A yawn escaped her lips awhile later. Reverently she closed the Bible, had her prayer, then headed for the tent.

The two men watched Loren leave the campsite the next morning. Getting into their old car they drove down the street far enough back to not scare the horses. Earlier they had picked out a possible ambush spot.

They decided on a place where tall trees stood on each side of the road and the brush was thick. The spot was on a hillside several miles out of town. They drove their car into some bushes well off the road. The road narrowed down into a one lane road for a short distance before turning into a well paved road. Both men grinned. Their prey was easy pickings, a woman on horseback riding alone.

. Now all they had to do was wait about thirty minutes for Loren to come. After ten minutes of waiting, both were dying for a cigarette. Did they dare smoke? The smell could warn her of someone's presence. They decided to take turns and smoke in the car. Just as one of them was finishing his cigarette, they heard Ranger's hooves hitting the stones on the road. Quickly he hurried back beside his friend. Peeking through the brush, they could see them coming. Almost here! Loren still had the small hill to climb before she reached the spot where they were hiding. For a short time Loren was out of the sight of the men.

Ranger stopped short before climbing the hill. His ears flipped back and forth picking up the whispering of the men ahead. Ranger also smelled the cigarette smoke. Before Loren could open her mouth to protest, Ranger turned to his left going leaving the main trail. A small animal trail provided just enough clearance for them to travel. Loren didn't question Ranger's decision. As they drew parallel to the main trail and could hear the men talking, she reached down and rubbed Ranger's neck. He had saved her again.

"She should have been here by now. Look out there and see if you can see her."

"She has to come this way. There are no other roads out of town. We need that money she is carrying. Are you sure you saw the man give her the money?"

"Yes. I'm sure. It would be hundreds. She wouldn't have spent all of it when she went shopping. We'll knock her off her horse and take the money. Do you have those handkerchiefs to put over our faces?"

"Right here."

Loren nudged Ranger forward. She had heard enough. Now she would go farther on this trail Ranger had found before getting back onto the main road.

Ducking low hanging branches, she let Ranger carry her to safety. This small incident made her aware that it was dangerous traveling alone.

Soon, they came out into a clearing at the fork in the road. She checked her map and took the right road heading back toward the valley and Andy. Now that she had a phone that worked, she still couldn't call him. Not knowing his last name, she couldn't use a phone book, either. Her timing was off just a day so far. Andy might consider that and wait a day before going to their meeting place. She still has three days of camping before she reached the valley meeting place. Ranger settled into his mile eating, shuffling walk. Loren settled down and once more enjoyed the scenery around her.

Familiar sights were located now. She would be able to travel quicker and know where she would end up at the end of the day. She was thinking about taking a different route for a change of scenery. The map showed several alternative routes that would still take her near the valley after three or four days of travel. Following a sharp turn to the left, Loren began a new route. Ranger didn't really care where they went, just so everyone was safe.

This new valley was larger than all the rest she had experienced. Very few homes were nestled about in the landscape. She even spotted several deer running across her trail. She would have to find new campsites and hope they were okay and safe. As she rode down through the valley, towards the main road, she saw a large tent was being set up. A sign advertised a revival meeting with services being held that night. Loren was curious. What was a revival?

Several men were working about the area clearing a large spot to put up the tent. A small motor home sat off to the side. She guessed that the man in charge stayed in it. Ranger stayed near a post while Loren walked over to the motor home. She knocked on the door. As the door opened, there stood the young preacher that had talked to her in the city. Surprise on both of their faces caused them to have a moment of silence.

"Hello. Where did you come from?" he asked as he stepped aside to let her enter.

"I am riding around trying to find myself. After talking to you several weeks ago, I have been seeking that peace God gives. I found it. You have helped me find Jesus."

"That is wonderful! Where are you going now?"

"I am heading back to the city, but am taking several days travel to do it. I was curious as to what a revival was."

"It is a gathering of Christians and non-Christians to lift their spirits and put fire under them, sort of speak. There are a lot of people who don't feel comfortable inside a Church but they would come to a tent. There are so many out there who need Jesus in their lives that we are trying to do that here. Can you stay?"

"Not really. I am on sort of a schedule with my food and the campsites that I know are there for me. I'm not familiar with this part of the country and I could get lost. My map from Waverly's KOA does not go very far into this particular valley area."

Here, I think I can help you out. We were in this area last week canvassing for this revival. A map was made of possible sites and the roads are shown on the map."

He went over to his desk and rummaged through a stack of papers. Pulling out a large sheet, he brought it over to the kitchen table. Spreading it out, he showed Loren where they were right then and the road for her to follow. He refolded the map and handed it to her.

"Let me show you around. I'm sure you have never watched a tent being raised."

"No, I haven't" Loren put the map into her pocket and walked across the grounds beside him. "I don't even know your name."

"I'm Ken Kinsey. I'm not really the main person in charge here, but I do some of the preaching. And you?"

"Loren Grayson."

"Any relation to Grayson Electronics?"

"My father. He visited me in Waverly or let me rephrase that. I found him at the hotel when I rode into town going to the KOA. We had dinner together."

The large tent was on its way up. Men stood on all of the corners ready to pull it up into place, then stake it down. Loren watched as they strained their muscles pulling the heavy canvas up toward the sky. Heavy mallets were swung down upon the huge metal stakes driving them into the ground. They had just finished getting everything completed when they heard motor bikes roaring down the road toward them. Four riders dressed in their leather outfits with helmets bore down on them. They had come to tear up the grounds and down the tent.

Ken grabbed Loren's arm and pulled her back to the motor home. He saw the danger and wanted to keep her safe. He was expecting trouble, but not like this.

"Stay here! They are here to drive us out and destroy what we have just finished."

Dirt was scattered as the bikers spun their bikes through the soft dirt. Workers scattered to get out of their way. When the bikers welded clubs, then things began getting serious. One biker tried to snag one of the tent's ropes to pull it loose while another went around on another side to do the same thing. Loren watched in horror. Why didn't the workers come to Ken's aid? One biker tried to swing his club at Ken to knock him down. Another biker spotted the horses. As he rode toward Ranger, Ranger looked back at him, his eyes wide with determination waiting the chance until he was a little closer to let him have it with one of his back feet. His hoof hit its target sending the rider down and the bike spinning off across the ground. Brownie turned his large rump into another rider's way and sent him flying over his handlebars. As one of the riders was getting up, he tried to grab Ranger's bridle. For this one time, Ranger forgot his ground tying training and turned on the man.

With teeth showing, he bit down on the man's arm. This man happened to be the leader of the attack. Instantly he yelled out to the others to beat it. He grabbed his now bleeding arm and got his bike. One of the workers had called the police and sirens could be heard coming down the road. Ken had a hold on one of the men and a couple of the workers now got the courage to come forth to help hold onto the men. Their bikes were down on the ground and of no use for a get- a- way. Several police cars stopped and blocked any escape by the men who still had their bikes. The bikers were rounded up and put into the squad cars. Their bikes were piled alongside the road for someone from the police department to come and pick up.

Ken hurried back to the motor home where Loren was standing. She gave him a weak smile.

"I'm okay. Wow! Does this happen very often when you set up at different places?"

"No, but this is the worst so far. Did you see your horses helping?"

Loren shook her head. "I was watching those men attacking you. Are you hurt?"

"No. I just wish my men had been more helpful. They probably know some of those men. Some are local help. How about something to drink before you leave. We have a vast assortment of cold drinks. I think your horses deserve a treat, too. I have some apples in the refrigerator we can give them."

"Thanks. They will appreciate that. They are such good horses."

They entered the motor home and sat drinking their cold soda. Ken continued telling Loren about his adventures he had had from his preaching with the tent ministry. When he had met Loren that day in the city, he had no idea that she would take the seed he had planted for her curiosity for God to take hold. Out of all the people he talked to, she was the only one who actually went all the way toward salvation and living the faith.

He followed her out to the horses. Loren gave them their treat, then checked their saddles. Ken watched as she mounted. Waving good bye, she turned Ranger and went on down the road. God was so good. He had made it possible for her to meet the young preacher again and thank him for guiding her in the right way. She offered up a prayer as she rode for his safety during his ministry. Reaching down, she rubbed Ranger's neck.

"You amaze me, Ranger. Sometimes I think you understand us humans and act accordingly. Well, we have used a lot of time. Let's keep moving."

That evening found the travelers on the edge of a lake. Loren thought about fishing, but she had no gear to do so. She found enough wood for a small campfire and fashioned a stick to roast a couple of hot dogs.

Seeing the sunset over the lake was a new and wonderful experience. The water on the lake turned the colors of the sunset sky. A slight breeze caused a rippling over the water. Frogs soon started to croak as the night sky followed the sunset. Loren climbed into her tent and slept.

During the night, she dreamed about Ken and Andy. She tried to picture herself with both men. Jeremy was not even in the picture. He could not compare to the two men she had met on her journey. Ken had light brown hair neatly cut and with hazel eyes that seemed to smile at you with the love of Christ shining through. A few freckles were spread across his nose. His figure was slight and wiry. Andy on the other hand was… Loren grinned. Just right.

He had called her a Bible thumper when she had told him she wasn't an angel. Maybe he wasn't a Christian. She would have to ask when they met again in a couple of days. Excitement in her grew. Just the thought of being with him made her blood hum.

The next morning Ranger was ready to go as he danced around a little before she had him saddled. Maybe she could try that trot again and ease him into a slow run. The air was chilly and both horses felt frisky. Even Brownie snorted as she was saddling up all the gear onto his back.

Mounting Loren patted Ranger's shoulder. "Okay boy, let's try a faster pace. I know you have been wanting to, so let's go!"

Ranger ventured out with his trot, then eased into his smooth rocking lope. Loren was surprised at the easy gait. Was this what she had been missing out on this whole trip? Wow! Even Brownie was enjoying the faster pace. The ground they were traveling on was good and firm. Easily the time flew by. Ranger was enjoying the run as was Loren. He could tell she had settled into his gait very well and was riding with him.

A car coming a little too fast down the road from the other way had Loren rein Ranger back to a walk. The car was weaving back and forth almost out of control. Loren reined Ranger far off the road out of the car's path. It went on by without an incident. Loren let the horses walk from then on. She grinned. She would be able to show Andy her accomplishments when she saw him.

A bridge over a small stream was in front of them. She led the horses down to the water for a drink. She got a bottle of cold water from her pack and drank it while the horses drank. She checked the saddle cinch, then remounted. They crossed the bridge and went on toward the mountain trail. She rechecked the map to make sure she was going the right direction and taking the right road. So far everything looked good.

When she stopped for lunch, she called her dad on the special phone. He answered. He had just finished a meeting and was putting away the papers in his file cabinet.

"Loren! What a surprise. Where are you?"

"Don't know, dad. I took a new route out of Waverly. This way is so beautiful. I stopped overnight at a lake that I'm sure is full of fish for you to catch. Don't know if I can find it again, but we can try. I let Ranger run with me. What a exciting feeling to run a horse. His gait was really comfortable, too. Oh, do you remember me telling you about that young preacher I met? I ran into him again yesterday. He was setting up a huge tent for a revival meeting. He is very interesting to talk to. You should have seen the size of his tent! Reminds me of that time you took me to the circus. It must have taken over two dozen men to put it up."

She didn't tell him about the bikers. No use getting her dad into a helicopter and coming after her to take her home where she would be safe. "Oh, Dad, I just looked on my map. I'm near a town called Kingly. I will take a route from there and head toward the valley I got lost in. Andy will meet me there. I'll visit with him for awhile, then start home. His place is only two days away. I was in the valley my second night out. I want to run my horse with his to feel what it would be like to race."

"Be careful, Loren. Your mother asked where you were. She didn't even know you were gone. I really need to get her straightened out on things. All she seems to do is spend my money on crap that doesn't mean anything. Her latest project is to change the garden around the pool. I had just paid big bucks to the landscaper to do all that just last year. Oh, well, I'm taking up your time with my problems. Are you still reading that Bible?"

"Oh yes, dad. Have you tried to, yet?"

"Um, no, Loren. Just can't seem to find the time. Maybe when you get home we can do it together."

"All right. See you soon." She turned off the phone and packed it away in the saddlebags. She got out an apple and split it up.

Both horses were eagerly awaiting their noon snack. Brownie licked his lips with his big tongue. Ranger started to do the same. Loren laughed. "You guys are pitiful! What are you going to do when we get back home and you won't get this royal treatment. I'm not even sure if I can buy either of you. I won't be able to take you both for sure." She rubbed Ranger's neck as he put his head down against her chest. She got a little teary eyed thinking about leaving Ranger when she got home to her 'boring' life. Her dad had offered a place in his company. Maybe having something to do would change her outlook on life. Only time would tell right now.

"Okay boys, let's rumble!" Easily she swung into the saddle and reined Ranger back toward the road. There was a KOA nearby and she wanted to get there tonight.

# CHAPTER 9

The KOA was located beside a small lake. Several boats were out on the water probably fishing. Loren found a campsite that offered enough trees to tie the horses between them like she usually did. In the office, they gave her a map of the area so she could route out her trip over to the forbidden valley. Everyone there seemed to know about the forbidden valley and the dangers that it held. Loren didn't tell them she had camped in the valley. She just told them the road past the valley was the road that she sought to take her home.

After traveling a couple of days, Loren finally reached the trail leading to the valley and Andy. She found the trail that Andy brought her out and started down it. Ranger helped with the directions. He was anxious to race that other horse. He felt his rider could handle a faster pace now. They were a day later than they had first told Andy they would be there. As they came around the valley, she watched several deer grazing on the valley floor. How could such a beautiful little valley be so evil? Sure there were wild animals about, but people had driven them out of the other parts of the valley and surrounding land. Where else could they go?

On the mountaintop overlooking the valley, Loren could see Andy's cabin. From that distance she couldn't tell if he was home or not.

Ranger stopped suddenly and nickered. Seconds later he was answered by another nicker. Andy came riding around a group of trees along the trail. He raised a hand in greeting. Ranger moved at a faster walk to catch up beside the approaching horse. Loren shoved her hat back on her head and wiped the sweat from her forehead. She wondered if she looked presentable as Andy came closer. Oh, what she would do for a hot shower and a make over!

"Howdy, little rich girl. How was your trip?"

"Wonderful. I had a great time. My dad even showed up in Waverly and we had dinner together. I cooked him breakfast at the campsite the next day. I didn't know your last name or I would have called you. I couldn't remember whether you said you had a cell phone or not."

"I do, but it doesn't work very well out here. If I need to call someone, I usually go in my jeep into town. Let's go back to the house. I'll bet you're tired."

"That I am. It will be good to be off a horse for awhile. The boys need a rest and roll in the dirt."

Andy laughed. "By the looks of all that trail dust on you, you could use a nice hot bath."

"Oh, that would be heaven! I do get showers at the KOAs, but nothing at the other campsites."

They rode together back to his cabin. He helped Loren remove the backpack off Brownie and get him into the corral.

Ranger was led into the corral and she proceeded to put her gear in his tack room beside the corral. She carried the backpack with her food into the house. Andy took her ice packs and put them into his freezer. Even though he was far out in the wilderness, he still had a way to generate electricity. It had taken him several weeks to string wire for power from an electric pole a mile away. He used the electric sparingly for only the refrigerator and once in awhile the lights. He couldn't offer Loren a hot tub, but the outdoor shower would work for her at the present time. She went into the bedroom and pulled out some clean clothes. She carried them out to the outside shower that Andy showed her. "Wait a few minutes for the hot water. I just turned on the generator. Don't worry about using too much. I have a large water tank."

As she stepped into the shower area, a large front room offered a comfortable place to change clothes. At the KOA their shower stalls were one after another with just a small area in the shower stall to change. This was almost a luxury.

When she came out, Andy had food on the table. Fresh fruit and sandwiches with cold ice tea with pickles and other stuff she hadn't been able to keep on her trip.

They sat in compatible silence after she said Grace. She wondered what his thoughts were. He seemed so distant and quiet.

"So, what have you been doing since I left you?" he asked, taking another bite of his sandwich.

"I have been having a wonderful time. It has had its exciting moments, though. Do you remember that preacher I told you about? Well, I ran into him again a couple of days ago. He is working as a revival preacher. They were setting up a tent when I was riding by. Some men on motorbikes were there trying to tear down the tent. The police came before they could do much damage. Old Ranger even got into the act. He kicked one guy off his bike."

Andy laughed. "I'll bet that was a sight to see."

Loren laughed and continued telling him about her adventures, but leaving out the part where she ran Ranger and liked it. She told him about the phone her dad had been working on and that it had worked out here in the wilderness. She showed it to him. Andy checked it out. He had heard about them, but it was the first one he had seen. He stood up and stretched. He didn't tell her that he invented parts for the phone she had. In a few weeks, he planned to visit her father's company to present them with a computer chip he had just finished making. With any luck, it would make the phone work a hundred percent better. He looked back over at Loren.

"How about a card or board game? No TV and I don't leave the lights on very long with my generator. I do have some electricity, but I keep that reserved for cooking and keeping the refrigerator going."

"Have you got Monopoly? Dad and I used to play that all the time when I was younger."

"Yep. Maybe tomorrow we can go for that run across the valley."

"I've been looking forward to that. I'm sure Ranger has been talking to your horse out in the corral about it, too. He's such a good horse. He has saved me several times from danger."

Loren helped Andy clear the table to get ready to play the board game. The pieces were down and the money divided. Andy flipped for who started. After an hour into the game, Andy knew he was getting beaten. She was a crafty player and knew how to stack up the motels on high rent properties on the board. Landing on one of her properties was like going bankrupt. The dice kept rolling numbers that was keeping him either in jail or on one of her high rental properties. Gritting his teeth, he was close to defeat. The excuse to feed the animals before dark gave him a short reprieve. Leaving the game, she followed him outside to help. Ranger and Brownie came to the fence to get their meal.

"Say Loren, ever milk a cow?"

"No. Is that easy?"

"Sure. Come on and give it a try." Andy got his stool and bucket. He already had the cow's lead line tied to a post. It was busily chewing its cud. Loren watched Andy sit on the stool and take a teat in each hand. Slowly with downward pulls, he squirted the milk into the bucket. He got up shortly and she sat down. He directed her hands around the teats and let her squeeze. Several seconds passed before any milk hit the bucket. She was scared, as well as the cow, so when a squirt hit the bucket a huge grin spread across her face. She had done it! She looked up at Andy. He grinned at her.

His city girl had milked a cow. Whoa! Where did that thought come from? She wasn't his and he wasn't sure if he wanted a woman to come into his life. Loren broke into his thoughts as she spoke. "How much do you take from her?"

"Oh, you can fill the bucket. I'll go feed the chickens and other animals here and about while you keep busy." He walked off chuckling to himself. He hadn't mentioned the ragged looking yellow tomcat that always showed up for a couple of squirts of milk.

Loren was squeezing away when she heard the meow that sounded more like a low growl of a wild animal. Slowly she turned her head and saw the big tom sitting there watching her. Somewhere she had heard or read about cats coming around at milking time to get some milk. She looked around on the ground for a bowl or pan of some sort, but couldn't find anything. When she looked back for the cat, it had moved up almost beside her. Well, she would try to squirt the milk directly to it, then.

Aiming the teat toward the cat, she squeezed. Milk sprayed out and the cat opened its mouth to catch the stream of warm milk. Loren held back the giggle as the milk covered its face. It was lapping it off almost as fast as she was squeezing the flow. It shook its large head, then turned away. It had had enough.

Loren stuck the teat back toward the bucket and continued to milk the cow. Andy had stood behind the building watching. He shook his head in amazement. This woman was something else! He watched the cat lumber off toward the back of the house where it would clean its face and rest until dinner was served.

Andy came back out from his hiding place and walked over to see her just finishing up with the bucket being almost full. He reached over and lifted it up while she got to her feet.

"Good job, Loren. Looks like some of it is missing."

"Oh sure. You can tell that? We had a guest for dinner. Want me to see if I can squeeze any more out of old Bessie, here?"

Andy laughed. "So the cat didn't scare you?"

"No. I figured out what he wanted. Are we about done out here? We need to get back and finish our game."

"There's no hurry." Loren laughed. She playfully slapped him on his arm. She had won the game! He was about ready to admit defeat.

When he suddenly made a grab for her, she squeaked out an eeek and dodged off to the right, and out of reach. Not really knowing what he planned to do, Loren took off running. Andy had set the full pail of milk down and was now intent on catching her. A short chase around the barn yard area ended with Loren snagged around the waist and pulled into his steel hard arms. Both were breathing hard from their running. Now they stood inches apart facing each other. Her eyes grew large as he slowly pushed a strand of hair back out of her eyes. Her breathing was now ragged with emotion. She watched the emotions change on his face as she stood still. Never before had she let a man get this close, let alone touch her. This feeling was new and didn't feel bad at all! Her arms were pinned to her sides, so she could not move if she had really wanted to. Andy's long dark eyelashes lowered as he closed the gap between their lips. With the lightest touch of a butterfly, they met and parted. She wanted more! Her eyes flickered open and looked into his dark blue ones. She slowly moved her tongue over her lips. Andy had released his strong hold on her, but just stayed close. He too, was breathing with difficulty. He had never had a kiss as sweet. It was like a potato chip; you couldn't eat just one. Loren had felt the strong arms release her, but she didn't want to move. Off behind her, the sun was starting to set in the West. It would be dark soon. Andy finally cleared his throat, put his hands on her shoulders turning her around to watch the sun going down. He wrapped his arms around her, holding her up next to him. Together they stood in silence watching the colors of the sky change.

As the sky darkened for night, they turned and walked back inside. The board game awaited their return. The excitement of the game was long past. They might as well pick it up and put it away. As Andy reached down to start putting the pieces away, Loren placed a hand over his.

"Hold on there, partner. I need to hear a few words of defeat or something to declare me the winner."

"Now you want me to grovel. I could turn the generator on and we can continue. We..."

"No, you need to save your gas. Tomorrow I want that race across the valley. Ranger thinks he can beat your old nag."

"What? No way! Okay, then. I will declare you the winner my dear lady."

He swept into a low bow and kissed her hand.

Loren laughed and clapped her hands in glee. She had won! She would win that race tomorrow, too. Her secret fast riding would pay off tomorrow. Hiding a smile that would choke a canary, she turned away to fiddle with putting the game away. They said their goodnights and separated for the night. Andy pulled the covers over him on the sleeping bag on the floor. He listened to Loren moving about in his bedroom preparing her nighttime ritual. It felt good to have company for a short time. After tomorrow, he didn't really know if he would see her again. He needed to finish working on his computer chip before he presented it to the president of Grayson Electronics.

With those few thoughts on his mind, he rolled over on his side and started to doze off. He heard Loren say 'ouch' and grinned. She had probably stubbed her toe on his table that he hadn't moved back against the wall after working yesterday.

The next day was starting out to be a great day. Loren could hardly hold back her excitement of the forthcoming race. She just knew that Ranger could easily beat Andy's horse. With breakfast eaten and all the animals taken care of, they saddled their horses. Loren rubbed her head against Ranger's. Whispering in his ear, she told him today was the big day they both had been waiting on. They both swung into their saddles and turned their horses toward the well worn trail leading down into the valley. As they reached the bottom, Andy stopped. Turning around in his saddle, he told Loren about the even terrain.

"The valley floor is fairly smooth and easy to ride fast. There is a sort of wide stream farther down that we can cross. It is the main part of the one where you camped that night. We can go slow to start and see how you get along. Ready?"

"I was sort of born ready. Lead the way." laughed Loren. Ranger tossed his head pulling on the reins. He wanted to go. She loosened the reins and he started his trot, then went into his smooth lope. Andy looked over and smiled.

"You are a natural. You have a good seat. Been practicing?"

"Whatever gave you that idea, dear sir? I am a spoiled brat, greenhorn, tenderfoot and whatever you might call me. An experienced rider, no. Practiced, yes. GO RANGER!" She nudged his sides and bent low over his neck.

With a leap of joy, Ranger left Andy and his mount in a cloud of dust standing still. Loren's laughter carried back in the wind to him as he urged his horse into a run to catch up. The thundering of their hooves coming up behind him made Ranger go that much faster. Andy was soon beside them matching stride for stride. He was now bent forward over his horse's neck intent on getting ahead and winning. As they inched ahead, he turned slightly in the saddle and waved. Loren loosened the reins and urged Ranger faster. They were gaining on him! Yahoo! The wide stream could be seen in the distance. Its water glistening in the sunlight. Andy reached the edge of the steam and waved farewell at Loren as he plunged into the water ahead of her water spraying all around them.

# CHAPTER 10

When Ranger reached the edge of the bank, he applied his brakes. With his front feet stuck straight out in front of him, Ranger skidded to a halt. Ranger came to a dead stop. Loren let out a small scream as she sailed over his head her arms and legs flaying the air as she turned a summersault and headed down into the water on her back. Ranger shook his head and nickered. 'Sorry, but I don't do water.'

Loren splashed water everywhere like a person doing a cannonball in a swimming pool as she hit the bottom. She landed on her rear-end with her legs sticking straight up into the air. She just missed a couple large rocks protruding near the muddy bank. She was now sitting in waist deep water with her legs now stretched out in front of her. When she had landed, the mud from the bottom lifted, making the water all around her muddy looking. Water streamed down from her head. She was completely soaked! Oh, did she feel like a mess!

Andy wheeled his horse around when he didn't hear her behind him. When he reached the bank, Loren was just wiping the hair back out of her eyes but still sitting in the water. His smile muscles started twitching. Holding back the laugh was really hard. Loren slowly got to her feet, water dripping from her hair and clothes. She took another swipe at her wet strands of hair and looked up on the bank at Ranger. He stood quietly looking at her. She could almost envision the halo over his head. She put her hands on her hips and stared at him. Ranger nickered.

She didn't know whether to laugh or yell at him. During the whole trip, she hadn't really put him through water. There had always been a bridge to cross on. As she walked back upon the bank, she twisted her shirt tail squeezing out the water. She did the same with her hair, then tied it back into the pony tail. Water sloshed in her shoes. She felt like laughing. This would be another great *Funniest Home Video Show* scene.

Andy waded back across the bank and dismounted. Crossing over to her, he offered her his handkerchief to wipe her face. Loren wrinkled up her nose at the thought of having to declare defeat. Andy took her hand and led her over to the shade of a large oak tree on the stream's bank. They sat down and would wait awhile for her to dry off some before riding on further. Several deer came bounding through the water to their side of the stream to run off down the valley floor. High up above them they could hear the screech of a hawk. Loren leaned back against the tree trunk and closed her eyes. The solitude of the place quickly soothed her nerves. After a short time, she turned to Andy.

"Andy, how is it that you can live like this in the wilderness all alone? Don't you want company?"

"You are with me, aren't you?"

"That is not the same thing. I will be gone probably tomorrow and we might not see each other again soon. My purpose of this trip has been met. I can now return to civilization and find a place in my father's company. My wanderings are done, I think."

"So did you find religion? I saw your Bible."

"It's not religion, Andy. It is a way of life. Being a Christian is trying to live like Jesus would want us to. I need to find out what He wants me to do and do it. God has been good to me. He has protected me through my whole journey so far. You have been a big part of it, too, Andy. I feel close to you."

"We can be friends, Loren. My peace with God will come, but not now. I hold too many bad memories of what He has done to me in the past. Until I can come to terms with that, then I can start believing again."

"Then I will continue to pray for you." Loren stood up and squeezed some more water from her shirt. She walked over to Ranger. He rolled his eyes at her being not sure what she would do to him. She patted his neck and checked the tightness of her saddle. With that done, she picked up the reins and mounted. Andy went to his horse and did the same. They rode farther into the valley to parts that Andy had never been before.

Several small animal trails were there to take if they so desired. Andy kept to the wider trail out in the open. He knew this valley and what the dangers were. Tall stone walls were soon before them. Trees along the cliff sides were stunted in growth. Andy suddenly pointed up. Loren followed his arm and saw the two mountain goats walking along the highest parts. After watching them disappear behind the rocks, Andy turned his horse back around toward home. Once more Ranger pulled on the reins. He wanted to run again. Andy's horse tossed its head in reply. Andy looked over at Loren for an okay.

She nodded and they were off once more. For awhile they ran side by side just enjoying being together. The wind rushed across their faces with the speed of the horses.

Loren leaned over Ranger's neck and urged him faster. Her breath was in short gasps, the speed seemed to take her breath away. Her sides hurt as if she had been running on foot. It was a feeling of actually running the race herself. Was that the feeling that the jockeys had in the horse races she had watched weeks ago? If so, she wished she was small enough to be a jockey. Then again she didn't. It was a dangerous sport. They rode different horses all the time and not really knowing what the horse was like before they got onto its back. This was more her speed. She could race Ranger whenever she felt like it either alone or find someone willing to run with her.

Andy slowed his horse as they reached the trail leading back to his cabin. Loren had easily won this race. He had really tried, but being heavier than her, his weight had caused him to lose. Loren reined Ranger around when Andy was not following her.

She had missed seeing the turn-off. She patted Ranger on his now wet neck and gathered up the loose reins. Sitting upright, she settled him into a slow walk and followed Andy up the trail. Back at the cabin, they both rubbed the horses down and put them into the corral. Andy handed her the bucket to milk the cow.

He put the saddles away and brought the cow outside, then tied her to the fence. Loren had the stool ready. She quickly ran off to clean up some before coming back to milk the cow.

Her clothes were getting dry, but stiff with the mud from the stream's bank. A nice hot shower was going to feel good in a few minutes. Andy fed the rest of the animals and went to turn on the hot water tank.

If Loren was leaving the next day, she would want to wash out her clothes. He wasn't sure how many outfits she had brought with her. As he was walking back toward the corral where she was, he saw the old cat sitting there waiting for his milk. He heard the joyful laughter of Loren as she shot the cat a stream of milk. He really did miss having someone around for company. The radio was really not much in the way of company. He could talk to it, but the radio could offer no response. His mind began to wonder about Loren. Could she be happy in this isolated spot he had chosen? No, she wouldn't. Maybe for a short time, but not permanently. Just thinking about returning to civilization scared him. Maybe a farm on the edge of a small town. Waverly was nice. People were friendly and the town had everything he would ever need. He would investigate some of these thoughts further. He hadn't even asked Loren how she would like living in this environment. Would she be happy here forever? The story of Ruth in the Bible nudged into his thoughts. She had chosen to go with her mother-in-law to her people rather than go to her own country where she had family. Several other Bible stories invaded his thoughts. He shook his head as if trying to erase them from his mind. What had Loren done to him? His dreams at night and his thoughts during the day were filled with her every since they first met at her campsite. She truly had looked like an angel when he had opened his eyes after being unconscious from his fall. He could see the changes in her from that time to now almost three weeks later.

She had taken on a journey of faith and had passed with flying colors. She had accepted Christ as her helpmate all the time, not just when things really got tough. He had been there before losing his fiancé. Maybe it was time for him to regroup and get back to God. He had several letters from his former minister asking for him to return and help with the youth program. That would be something Loren would probably like to do. Loren's laughter broke into his thoughts. The cat had actually gotten its face covered with milk. Loren had purposely squirted milk a little higher to get its reaction. It shook its head and ambled off toward the house. Loren bent her head and tried to whistle a happy tune. Andy shook his head. She couldn't carry a tune and probably even with the help of a ten gallon bucket. He walked out and helped her with the full bucket of milk. She grabbed the stool and put it away. She took the basket of eggs he carried up to the house while he took care of the milk.

Loren went to gather her clean clothes and headed out to the shower. Her clothes were now stiff with the drying mud. She bet that she looked a mess. She had seen Andy get the hot water going and it should be ready by now. As she showered, she washed her muddy clothes right there in the shower water. Now she would have a clean change to take on the trip. Leaving in the morning made her sad. She wanted to stay longer. With her wet clean clothes hanging up on the clothes line, she went into the house. Already the smell of beef stew assailed her nose. She really hadn't realized that she was hungry. That long run had tired her out.

Andy showed her how to make biscuits from scratch. With them in the oven, she set the table.

"I'll be leaving in the morning, Andy. Is there a trail I can take going in the other direction?"

"Sure. You can follow my jeep tracks out behind the cabin. Uh, Loren, do you think you could live in the wilderness like this?"

"I'm not sure, Andy. Are you asking me to?"

"No, we don't know each other well enough for that kind of a commitment. I'm just feeling you out. We come from different ways of life. I chose this way of life to leave all my past problems behind me. We all have skeletons in our closets that we don't want people to know about. I'm not ready to leave the safe haven I have made here to face the world and God. I was just curious if you could live like this alone with nature.

I realize that you did manage to make your two week trip, but there were people and other things you faced, but not totally alone like me. Forget it. I'm just going around in circles." He started to turn around toward the table.

Loren put a hand on his arm. "No, Andy. I think I understand what you are asking me. I do require the presence of people. Being here in the short time that I have been, has been nice, but I don't think I could stand the solitude for more than a couple weeks at a time. Being out of touch with phones, modern conveniences and shopping, I would go bonkers. Sorry."

Andy turned toward the fireplace to hide his disappointment. She could not live here. Maybe she was right. It was too soon to even bring something like that up. If he could compromise, maybe, just maybe. He felt better right away. There was just something about this woman that was different. She didn't flaunt her riches like most rich people did. True, she didn't work in a job, but she had just finished a journey that no other female he knew would have attempted alone. He would give her his name and address so she could correspond with him after she got home, if she wanted to. They spent the rest of the evening in front of the fireplace nibbling on popcorn and drinking hot chocolate. The weather had turned a little cold and the fire and company felt good to both of them. Andy talked about things he had done around in the area, but nothing crucial about his past. He didn't know how this relationship would take him, but he wanted to see Loren again. He had seen the almost hidden brand on Ranger's hip and knew where he had come from. Andy ached to see his parents again. Would he be welcome? He doubted that Ranger or Brownie would remember him for he was a lot younger when he left home. He got up and put another log on the fire. He hoped this cold front would soon pass and not cause Loren any trouble traveling back home. She hadn't even left his sight and he was already missing her!

Morning came far too soon for both of them. Loren was busy packing her leftover food she had bought in Waverly. Andy gave her some snacks he had on hand. Stepping outside, the cold air blasted them.

"Burrrr. It's going to be a cold morning. I'm glad I have extra warm clothes."

"You will be okay. Now that you know how to ride faster than a slow walk, Ranger will take you home faster. Maybe you can get a good sheltered spot at your campsite tonight. Here is my address and cell phone number when you get into an area where you can call. Let me know how you are doing and write me. I have enjoyed having you here, Loren." He took her face between his hands and gently lowered his to kiss her goodbye.

The kiss was one of longing and desire, but neither would go any further. They were friends, not lovers. Andy hugged her close savoring the smell of her. He would miss her. He put his hands on her shoulders and gently turned her toward the corral. He went into the barn and brought her gear out of the tack room. Brownie was caught and brought outside the corral to prepare the packsaddle. Andy brushed Brownie before tacking him. Ranger trotted around the corral, anxious to get started. Snorting, he did a few crow hops and bucked around kicking up his heels to get warmed up. It was cold! He was waiting at the gate when Loren came to get him. He shoved his nose into her chest, almost knocking her over. She laughed and scratched his neck. She brushed him good before putting on the saddle blanket and saddle.

Andy handed her the saddlebags and she put them over Ranger's rump. Andy tied down the one side while she did the other to keep them in place.

"I guess I am ready. Thanks for everything, Andy. I will call you when I get to my campsite tonight. Dad gave me an experimental phone to use that his company is working on. It has a wider range of service."

"Good." He kissed her again and stood back while she mounted. Gathering up the reins, she turned toward the back of the cabin where he had shown her the road. Andy patted Brownie on his rump as the horse walked past him.

Slowly she rode past the shed, the barn and on down the road toward the main road that was about two miles away. Ranger tossed his head anxious to move faster.

"You can wait. This is a new road." She patted his neck and sat back up in the saddle. She let her mind drift over the events of her journey. She would definitely pray for Andy and his reluctance to return to God.

With Ranger's faster pace on the familiar road, Loren made it to her first campsite in plenty of time to set up camp. So many memories from this first spot. She unsaddled both horses and tied them to the rope. She then found the empty bucket she had used the first time and filled it full of water. Everything was the same, only this time she knew what she was doing. She began preparing her evening meal. Andy had packed a couple thick roast beef sandwiches for her and a couple of cold sodas.

In her excitement to leave early the next morning, she just spread out her sleeping bag back under a tree on a thick bed of pine needles instead of setting up the tent. Her thoughts went forward to working with her father in the company. What kind of job would she be doing? What could she do with so little skills. She would take a tour into every department and check out each possibility. She was sure she didn't want a desk job. There was no real challenge in that position that would satisfy her.

As the sun started to go down, she placed her Bible across her lap and called Andy on her dad's phone. He picked it up on the second ring.

"Hey, traveler. How's it going?"

"I'll be back at the stables late tomorrow afternoon and then the short drive home. I'm already feeling depressed. This has been a wonderful trip. Wish you were here."

"Really? Same here. We could do another Monopoly game."

Loren laughed. "Do you really want to get beaten that bad?"

"Oh, you cut right to the heart! And you left me all alone with no one to practice with. It is not a game of solitaire. Call me again when you get home. Okay?"

"Sure. I'll be praying for you, Andy."

"I… I appreciate that, Loren. I really need to work at this problem of mine. I have a lot of reconciling to do."

"Give everything over to God and He will help you through the hard parts. It might seem hard, but it really isn't. Look at me. I managed and I had never heard of Jesus Christ before as a person, just swear words used around in my social circle. It will be your journey of faith. I'd better sign off and reserve the batteries. There is no electricity here at this campsite."

"Okay, Loren. I will talk to you in a couple of days. I'm off to Waverly tomorrow."

"All right, Andy. See ya." She pushed the off button and set the phone down. Turning the pages in her Bible, she found some passages that she wanted to read before it got too dark. The fading sunset did not disappoint her. It was just as beautiful as it was that first night out. She waited until the last of the lavender colors had blended into the darkened night sky. Slowly she walked off to the restroom to get ready for bed.

She stopped at the picnic table and climbed upon the top. Facing the western sky as it slowly turned dark for night, she prayed. This trip was so wonderful and invigorating that it overwhelmed her what God could do for her. She had changed from a boring socialite into a… what would she call herself now? Loren chuckled. Would her so-called friends look upon her as a 'now common' woman? She still had her wealth and beauty. Her body was well toned and muscular from hours in the saddle riding. She would never be the same again. With a final look at the darkened sky, she climbed down from the table and slipped into her sleeping bag.

# CHAPTER 11

Morning found her up bright and early. Ranger and Brownie were ready to go. Eagerly they devoured their grain and drank the water she brought to them. Soon they were saddled and everything packed away on Brownie. She felt excitement as she headed back toward the trail to the stables and home.

Joel had just finished feeding up all the other horses when he saw Loren coming down the road. He hoped she had a good time and didn't have much trouble along the way. He raised a hand in greeting as she rode up and stiffly dismounted. What a trip! It was over. She led both horses over to the hitching post and looped the reins over it.

"How did you do, Loren?"

"I had a fantastic time, Joel. I want to buy Ranger. He is the most amazing horse I have ever encountered.

He has only one hang up, though. He will not go through water."

Joel chuckled. "I hope you weren't going very fast when you found that out."

Loren laughed. "I was. I was racing someone and we came to a stream and he just threw on the brakes and I went sailing over his head and into the water. I think he even laughed at me."

"You must not have had very much water to cross on your journey."

"I did, but there were bridges to go across. Let me unsaddle them and help you put them away. I bet you already have everyone fed up by now."

"Yep. Come on. I'll help."

Together they worked undoing all the straps and gear. Ranger shook himself as did Brownie. They were home. Joel brushed Brownie while Loren did Ranger. Inside the barn, they were put into their stalls and fed their grain. Loren threw hay over into the corners of their stalls. Back outside, she put all her gear into her car.

"I'll come back out tomorrow and tell you all about my journey. Right now, a hot bath sounds mighty good. I'll see you later."

"I'll be here. Come any time. Maybe the Misses can fix you a nice cup of coffee and some of her cinnamon buns."

Loren licked her lips with the memory of those cinnamon buns back on her trip. "I would really enjoy that. Bye Joel."

The car started right away. She backed it up and put it into gear. Soon, too soon she was back in the city. She had almost forgotten how to drive in traffic. Two weeks away from it and it was almost like starting over. Through several turns and down familiar streets, she arrived home.

Her side of the garage door opened at the touch of the button in the car. Unpacking her gear, she stacked it neatly on the shelves. She carried the saddlebags into the house so she could unload the cold packs and food she hadn't eaten. Sally, the maid, met her as she entered the kitchen. She set her cleaning supplies down and came over to help Loren put away her things. Loren bit her lip to keep from making a snide remark. She often put Sally down when she wanted her way in the kitchen. The change in her life prevented her from making cruel remarks

"Sally, let me do this. While I was gone, I learned a little on how to take care of myself."

"This I must see." said Sally in her Spanish accent. She stood back and crossed her arms in front of her as she leaned back against the counter. Loren was quickly getting confused. She wondered how Sally knew where everything was kept.

After a few minutes of not getting things back where they belonged, Loren turned toward Sally and offered her a grim smile. "I guess I really don't know my way around your kitchen. Will you show me where these things should go? I'll put them in place. Just lead the way."

Sally was astonished by Loren's reaction. Was this *really* Loren? She looked like her, but surely did not act like her old self. Her body was tanned and looked healthy like she had spent days at a spa.

Soon everything was in their rightful place. Sally went back to her cleaning and Loren walked on through the house heading for the stairway. She stopped at its bottom and lovingly ran a hand over the highly polished wood of the railing.

Looking up, she remembered all the times as a small child trying to get her parents to allow her to slide down its slick railing. Feeling almost like a child right then, she was almost tempted to try it. No, she was grown up. If she wanted a wild ride, she would go and ride Ranger toward a water crossing! Laughing out loud, she mounted the steps two at a time. She was home!

Minutes later found her deep in a frothy bubble bath leaning back against the top of the tub. If there ever was a luxury she had to do without, this would not be one of them. Taking a deep breath, she slid down under the water. This was close to heaven. Coming back up, she shook her head like a dog, laughing as the water sprayed everywhere. There was a maid to clean this up, too, but would she put forth the effort to try to do it herself. Wrapping up into a large soft towel, she dried herself.

After she was dressed, she put all her dirty laundry into a basket and carried it downstairs to the laundry room. Another servant was there folding sheets they had just finished drying. One came forth to take her basket. Reluctantly she let her take it and went back upstairs to finish what she needed to do. She had yet to find her mother and let her know she was home.

Loren found Paula, her stepmother, in her bedroom chambers. One of the servants was doing her nails. Loren looked down at her short broken nails. Maybe she could at least try to repair them while she talked to her mom.

"Hi, Mom."

"Loren, dear. Where have you been these last couple of weeks? Your father said you had gone camping with a horse? How utterly out of character for you. Jeremy has called several times asking about you."

Loren sat down beside her. She first addressed the servant. "Kerri, is there any hope for my fingers? A couple nails broke off when I was tightening my saddle so I just cut the others short. I think they have grown out some."

"Oh my! Those beautiful hands! Look at those ghastly calluses! Here. Soak them in this solution while I finish your mother's."

Loren did as she asked. She answered her mother's questions and began to tell her a little about her adventure. When she reached the part about reading her Bible and praying, her mother stopped her.

"We won't talk about religion in this house. God does not have a place here."

"Why not, mother? Being a Christian is not a religion. It is a way of life and the only way a person can get to heaven is through Jesus Christ. Why do you not want God in this house?"

She tried to explain the plan of salvation and her experiences along the trail with God's help. Her mother completely shut her off. She dismissed Kerri and left Loren sitting there alone. She had buried her past and no one, not even the stepdaughter was going to find out her shady past. Loren's father had found her in with high society, but she had fought to gain entrance into the cream of the crop. Both of her parents had long been split up and had left her almost in the streets to fend for herself.

Paula had been resourceful in that she went ahead and finished school and graduated at the head of her class. A friend of her mother's had helped her go to a finishing school to gain poise and airs to gain access to the high society she craved. She had done it all on her own. She didn't or hadn't needed God or anyone else to get herself to the top. This stepdaughter was spoiled. She didn't do a thing to further her career in seeking a rich man to marry and live well within her means. Paula had met Loren's father at a New Year's Eve party and had gone after him once she learned how rich he was. Through a whirling courtship of wining, dining and traveling to Europe, she married him. Now, this daughter was trying to bring God into the picture. God had not been around her when she was growing up and really needed Someone to depend on. None of her childhood friends took her to Sunday School and told her about God. So how was she to know what a loving God was? She arched her eyebrows at Loren just before she left the room. The door closed silently behind her. Loren pulled her hands out of the solution and dried them. So much for a manicure. Loren returned to her bedroom. There, she took out the worn Bible and began to read in Psalms. She had found comfort there and that was what she needed right then.

Her reunion with her father that evening was exciting as well as comforting. He embraced her rejection from the mother with open arms. Together they talked well into the night about her many adventures and experiences. The mother heard them laughing behind closed doors of the study. Just a little tiny bit, she wished she had that closeness with Loren. Maybe she could have if she had not changed so much over the last couple of weeks and got 'religion'. Even her relationship with her husband was not the greatest. She was beginning to wonder why she even married him. Oh, it was the millions of dollars that he was worth. That had to be it. He really wasn't that bad looking either. They had gone to many social events where they were recognized as high society. That alone was worth something, wasn't it? She tossed the Glamour magazine aside and reached for the TV remote. She was getting bored. There had to be a party somewhere they could attend.

When she looked up, Loren and her father was coming out of the study. He had his arm draped across her shoulders. They had decided that she would come to the office with him the next morning and check out a possible job for her to do in the company.

"I'm going to bed, Paula. Care to join me?"

"I might as well. There's nothing around here to do." she flipped the off button on the remote and set it down on the couch. She stood and followed them to the stairwell. One of the servants turned out the lights as they reached the top of the stairs.

"Good night, Loren. See you at breakfast. We are eating inside tomorrow."

Loren laughed. "It will be a real treat not to cook for myself tomorrow. Night mom. Night, dad."

As she retired to her room, she wondered if Andy was still awake. She found the sheet of paper he had written his address and phone number on. Dialing the number, she waited for his voice. Talking to him was like being back out on her adventure. He was truly pleased to hear from her and hoped she would do well in the company. Andy didn't tell her he was seeing a realtor the next day to look at some property near Waverly.

He had several go-rounds with God, with God winning. His fiancé Margo, was now in the past where she belonged. Now, if he could reconcile with his parents and Margo's, he would be clear to love again and start over. Loren had helped tremendously when she was there with him. He knew she was only a new Christian, but her faith was strong. She would go far if she could get in with some solid Christians near where she lived. Being among fellow believers was very important to a young Christian. They would be there for support and build her up when she was feeling low. Sleeping that night was easier for him. He was moving forward once more. Tomorrow he would travel to Waverly and check on some property near there. He was anxious to please Loren, knowing now that he loved her. Being close to town and stores, might make it easier for her to accept his proposal. Already in his mind, he had the way he wanted to play it out. In a way, he could hardly wait to tell her. He knew though, he couldn't rush her. She was still timid and naïve regarding love making. Slow and easy. That would be the way he would go. Like his dad always told him about training a horse. You needed to gain their trust in you before you tried to change them.

# CHAPTER 12

Loren followed her father around the company from the bottom area that was the mailing and shipping department to where they now were in the assembly department. When she passed the designing areas, she stopped and watched one of the workers draw out a diagram of something. As she watched, she saw him compare what he was working on to another drawing in front of him on the drawing board. He made a few changes and continued with his work.

"Dad, what is this supposed to be?" Her dad came back over to the table where she was standing. The man doing the drawing stopped his work, being a little embarrassed by the sudden attention.

Mr. Grayson looked at all the drawings before he answered Loren. "It is a drawing of another prototype of the phone I gave you. When he has it finished, it will go to the parts department and they will make the components that will make it work."

"Can I see that section?"

"Sure. This way."

They weaved around the various tables with different stages of things being assembled. Tiny wires and parts covered the table with the soldering iron.

Loren looked at each table, getting interested in what was going on with the work in progress.

At the last table, they stopped and examined the parts being put together. Loren picked up a couple of pieces and examined them. In just a few simple moves, she had part of the phone put together. The workers around them was astonished at her skill. The boss's daughter, no less! Loren kept putting the pieces together. The worker there showed her the wires to attach and helped her tighten the screws. In just a few more minutes the two of them had everything together like she thought they should go. Someone handed her some batteries already charged to put into the phone. Loren looked up at her father. She pushed the 'on' button. Some static sounded, then as she turned the knob, it became clear. She dialed the phone number of one of her friends and was excited when the phone began to ring. No one was at home, but their answering machine kicked in.

Embarrassed by the sudden attention, Loren turned it off and placed it back on the table. Her face reddened at all the attention she was receiving. Everyone clapped. She had found her place in the company! This assembly place was not as low as the shipping department, but one of a skilled position. She hadn't realized that her talent of a somewhat photogenic memory would ever be useful. For years she had stuck that knowledge back in the recesses of her brain never to use in anything useful. Her father put his arm across her shoulder and smiled.

"Looks like you are talented in the assembly department. Let Troy take you under his wing and let you work with him for the rest of the day. Let's see what you can do. I'll see you at noon. We can have lunch in the cafeteria."

"All right, dad." Excitement leaped through her. She had found a spot where she could be useful. She could hardly wait to tell Andy.

Troy guided her over to the other side of the table and pulled out a new apron for her to wear. Even though she wore every-day clothes, she would eventually get dirty.

Lunchtime found Loren tired from standing in one spot and hungry enough to eat whatever was in her sight. Troy had been a good teacher and was patient when she made her beginner's mistakes. One of the other women workers showed her where the ladies room was and went with her to the cafeteria where everyone ate. One of the workers even offered to bring her something if she wanted to sit down and be waited on. She shook her head.

"No thanks. I want to be an equal worker. All my life I have lived with servants waiting on me. I need to learn to fend for myself. Thank you."

The workers were pleased by her friendliness and willingness to learn from the ground floor. She tried to make friends by being open to their help. After the first day, all the people she worked with knew where she stood. One even ventured to ask her if she was a Christian.

"Yes, I am. I found Jesus Christ on my horseback trek across country for two weeks. He really is a great comfort and I am enjoying reading the Bible and learning more about Him."

"Your father has changed some since you left. He has been more lenient with some of us saying grace at the table and praying for a fellow worker who is sick or injured. Maybe by you coming to work with us, some of the other stiff policies will be changed."

"Thank you for talking to me. I will check out the worker's manual."

Time passed quickly and soon the end of the work day was over. Loren folded her apron and placed it under the table. Heading to the ladies room, she washed her hands and headed for the parking lot to her car. Once inside, she rested her head on the steering wheel. With a contented sigh of relief, she smiled in the rear view mirror. She had made it! Now if she can just keep up with her new job and help where she is needed.

Relaxing in the bathtub full of soapy bubble bath, Loren leaned back against the back and let her muscles relax. She was anxious to call Andy and see what he was doing and to tell him about her wonderful first day at work. Won't he be surprised. She was still a little rich girl, but now she could actually amount to something. She immediately thanked God for every blessing He had given her that day and now slowly pulled herself upright in the tub. Wrapping herself in a large fluffy towel, she dried off. Slipping her feet into her flip-flops, she padded across the hall to her room. One of her servants had laid out some evening clothes to wear between bedtime. Wrinkling up her nose at the expensive looking sundress, she replaced it into her closet and rummaged through to find a more suitable outfit.

Now, she twirled in front of the full length mirror dressed in her peach colored pants and large sleeved open collar blouse. Her damp hair was pulled back into a ponytail. Still wearing the flip-flops, she headed into the hallway and to the stairs. Voices in her parent's room caused her to slow down. Not really meaning to eavesdrop, she heard the argument. Her mother was protesting putting Loren into the work place like an ordinary person. Calmly, at first, her dad was trying to explain why Loren was being taught the family business. Paula didn't want anything to interfere with her plans for Loren. She wanted Loren to reconcile with Jeremy and plan a future possible marriage of the two. Society was where Loren needed to be, not hidden in the bowels of a computer workplace.

Loren tiptoed on past the bedroom door and went downstairs. She would eventually hear about all of the outcome sooner or later. As she walked toward the kitchen door, she could smell the fragrant smells of Sally's cooking. It would be good to be able to sit down to a good meal without cooking it herself. Jane was at the table placing the plates and silverware around at the settings. She looked up and smiled shyly at Loren. Loren nodded a greeting with a smile and walked on toward the library. She was home and now to keep busy. She sat at her dad's desk and dialed Andy's number.

Andy answered on the third ring. He was excited to hear from her.

"Loren, how are you?"

"Andy, I have finally found my niche in life. Dad took me on a tour of the company today and I got a job working in a section of the assembly department. I found out that I have what people call a photogenic memory."

She went on to tell him about the phone that she put together and how well the workers accepted her as their equal. She told him about meeting the stable man and being invited to come out any time to ride and possibility share a meal. As she was ending their conversation, she heard the dinner bell summoning the family to the table. Softly she laughed. So much seemed different to her since she had come home from her journey. Lots of little things stuck out where she never saw or thought of them before. Her ladies who served her in the home needed to be addressed now as equals. Boy, would her step-mom have a cow! She put down the phone and went out into the foyer. Paula was now making her 'grand' entrance down the stairs with her dad right behind her. Loren held back the chuckle of amusement. Before, she really hadn't taken all this pomp and circumstance seriously. Did Paula really expect to do this every night?

Now seated at the table, Loren looked at her dad. Did she dare ask to say grace?

She felt the urge to do so. Why stop a new habit now that she was home?

"Dad, do you mind if I say a table grace before we eat?"

Mr. Grayson looked at his daughter. He knew of the drastic change in her and knew she would continue to grow closer to God. He gave her a slight nod and avoided looking over at Paula for her reaction.

He had put in a hard day at work and didn't need more confrontation from her, especially in front of the servants. He bowed his head as she started the prayer, hoping Paula would play along. He could tell they were on a rocky road, but they would survive. The smell of the wonderful meal reached his nose as the food was now being passed by the servants.

Paula did give Loren a look that would kill, but she ignored the look. Her mother would no longer reduce her to a meek little step-daughter. Paula watched Loren and instantly noticed the change in her. It was not just the outward appearance, either. She was tanned from being outdoors those two weeks, but something inside her had changed. Curious, but not curious enough to ask here in front of Gray and the servants, she kept quiet. Her thoughts went on in the days ahead when she could get Loren and Jeremy back together. All this 'shop' talk at the table was boring. Throughout her whole marriage to Gray, she had not really cared about how he made all his money, just as long as he would give her whatever she wanted. Church? What had she missed in her thoughts of other things. Just the word 'Church' jerked her out of her reverie. Paula's head jerked up from her plate and she stared at Gray.

"What's this about church?"

"Loren and I thought we might attend a church service Sunday. Would you like to join us?"

"We go to church on occasion, Gray. That big one down-town where the Smithfields and Jamesons go."

Gray reached over and took Paula's hand in his. Lovingly he smiled at her.

"We are changing our routine, dear. We don't need the prestige of our station in life any longer. We now need to learn more about God and His Son Jesus."

"You have *got to be kidding*! Gray, I will not stand for it. God has no place in this house! We are doing fine without Him!" violently Paula shoved back from the table, almost upsetting the chair she was sitting in. Throwing down the napkin onto her plate, she whirled and stomped out of the room.

Loren looked at her father with saddened eyes. Tears threatened to fall. Maybe it was too soon. Her step mom was not ready to accept the sudden change that she had. She continued to eat the meal, although she no longer had an appetite. Her father reached over and patted her shoulder, then continued his meal. Words were not needed right then.

With the meal over, the servants came out and cleared the table. Gray headed off to his den and Loren remained undecided as to where she wanted to go. Slowly she wandered around the house and eventually ended up in the garden. Taking a seat on one of the cement benches, she sat down staring off into the many rose trellises now full of bloom. Turning slightly, she glanced back up at the house. A light in her mother's room flashed on and she could see her moving across the room. What would it take to set her step mom's heart right? Loren dropped her head into her hands as her elbows rested on her knees. Groaning out a prayer for help and direction, she let the tears fall. She hadn't really realized how much her step mom hated religion. She seemed to be okay when they attended the large church downtown. The minister's message was about God, but telling everyone that being good and being a friend to everyone was all that they needed to enter heaven. She had thought that, too, before her horseback journey. Now she realized the importance of really knowing Jesus and what He can do in a person's life.

Loren wiped the tears from her eyes and blew her nose. She watched the clouds coming together to create night. From where she was sitting, she couldn't see the sunset, but she wished she could. Tomorrow she would try to locate a good place to watch the sun go down and maybe get her dad to sit with her. Somewhere in the space of their lot there had to be a place free of trees to block out the sun going down. The night crickets and other insects of the night began their serenade to Loren. A stiff breeze swept over her causing goose bumps to form on her arms. Rubbing her arms vigorously, she warmed up, but not enough to stay outside any longer. Slowly she stood and stretched, then turned back toward the house. Tomorrow as another work day.

# CHAPTER 13

Andy stood in front of the nice freshly painted farmhouse. Behind the house stood a well built barn and several out buildings. The pasture fences needed repairing before he could turn his animals loose. The cat was soon at home in the barn along with a female who had already lived there. She had stayed behind when the previous owners moved. She was not pleased by the intrusion, but soon accepted him as long as he kept his distance. She had a young litter of kittens hidden in the hay loft. She knew other male cats would kill the offspring if they were not his. Being a worldly cat, the old Tom left her alone. He did his exploring of the area, quite pleased with his new home.

Andy moved some of his furniture into the house keeping it in one of the rooms while he went about repairing windows and cracked walls.

He wondered if Loren would like this place. He couldn't seem to get her off his mind. Once he had come to terms with his past, she showed up in his thoughts more often. She seemed excited about her new place in her dad's company.

He was surprised, too at her knowledge of the intricate parts of the phone they were assembling at the company. He picked up the drawings of a new part he had been working on for her father's company. They were to send a complete phone kit to him for experimental use. He had just sent off his new address to them that morning.

Several weeks later, Andy was completely moved into the farmhouse. Some of the local neighbors helped him put up new fence around his property. Now his two horses and the cow had plenty of running room. Watching the horses frolic out in the pasture made him long for a long ride. What if he rode to his dad's stables and surprised Loren? He hadn't heard from her since that first night, so he knew she was busy working. The weather was good. Why not ride from here like she did? He had a copy of her map showing all of her campsite spots. Excitement grew and soon he was planning the horseback journey. Just like Loren, he prepared all of the necessary items he needed, but carried everything on his horse. At least he was going to until his pile of equipment grew to an overwhelming amount. His other horse accepted the packsaddle and stood while he arranged everything. He would leave the next day. Right now he was practicing. The horse's feet were checked and soon everything was in readiness to leave the next morning.

His next door neighbor agreed to take care of the cow and other animals for him. Andy swung up into his saddle and turned the horses toward his cabin and the valley.

He could stay there the second night out. Loren had camped between his farmhouse and the valley. As he rode with a loose rein, he checked the map and found the campsite. It was near that farrier's home. He found it and settled down for his first night out.

His tent was put up in record time. Grinning to himself he wondered how she had done her first night out with her tent. He then remembered her telling him about that it would have made that show *The Funniest Home Videos.*

After picketing the horses on the long rope, he got them water and went about getting his first meal started. He didn't need a book on How to Survive the

Wilderness. If he had a mind to, he could have written the book. Like Loren, he enjoyed the sunset that night. Before it had gotten dark, he took out his worn Bible. Where had Loren said she had found peace? It was in Psalms. Opening the Bible in the middle, Psalms was right there. The comfort for him though, was not there. A slight breeze ruffled back the pages and he ended up in Isaiah. With Christmas only a few months away, he found references to Jesus in Chapter nine verse six. He remembered that Isaiah also prophesied Jesus' suffering in Chapter 53. Oh, could he regain his faith? Maybe this could be his journey of faith like Loren. He closed the Bible after reading the passages and put it into his pack.

Late afternoon found Andy trudging along on the mountain trail toward the cabin. Rain was pelting down on them soaking him to the skin. He had forgotten to pack a rain slicker. With everything already moved to his new home, he would have to sleep on the floor. At least the horses could be inside the barn. He got them inside the barn and unsaddled. Finding some old towels, he wiped them both down before making a run for it to the house.

Fresh hay was spread out for them to lay on and eat along with the grain he had brought with him.

Inside the empty cabin he tossed his gear on the floor. There was still dry wood he could burn in the fireplace for some heat and light. He pulled out an old rug to put before the fireplace and sat down Indian fashion. Two hot dogs were stuck on a stick and roasted over the nice warm fire. He pulled the flip top on a small can of pork and beans, then grabbed an almost warm soda from his pack. In two more days he would be at the stable. He would have to see about renting a car to go into the city after getting to the stable. He wanted to spend some time with his parents first, though. He had a lot of explaining to do and bonds to patch. He needed to see Margo's parents, too. He hadn't talked to them since the funeral. Boy, did he have skeletons in his closet!

As the storm raged outside, he spread out his sleeping bag and prepared to go to sleep. Sometime during the night, he heard a loud crack of lightening. Jerking upright in the sleeping bag, he scrambled out and stood up. Going to the window, he could just barely see where a tree had fallen across the corral fence. As the sky lit up again, he saw that the barn was safe. He could thank God for the rain and making him put the horses in the barn. Otherwise, they would have been in the corral and probably gotten hurt or killed. Like Loren had told him. God was watching over him as well as He had for her. Right then, he bowed on his knees and prayed; thanking God for watching over him and asking

Him to keep him close. Now, he felt better. Sliding back into his sleeping bag, he drifted off to sleep.

Morning found him outside getting ready to move on. The tree top had just scraped across the side of the barn leaving very little damage. Most of the corral itself was damaged where the tree had leveled the boards. One more campsite before reaching the stables. If he pushed the horses into a faster pace, he could make it by nightfall. He decided to do that. He knew Loren had walked Ranger all the way, thus not making very good time. He stopped just a short time for a lunch break and then pushed on.

Back at Joel's stable, Ranger trotted toward the front of the pasture, his ears pricked forward. He heard another horse coming on the road. With a snort, he began pacing along the fence. Joel came out and watched him.

"What's going on, big boy? What do you hear?"

Ranger came up to him and shoved his chest with his nose. Whirling about, he pranced around, then came back to stand still, with ears forward. He nickered and was soon answered. Joel looked toward the road but seeing nothing. Soon, the horse and rider came into view. Was that Andy? What was he doing here? Joel left the fence and walked around toward the front door of the barn. That was where he stood when Andy rode up. He turned his horse toward the hitching post and stiffly dismounted. He saw Ranger tossing his head on the other side of the fence by the barn. Andy tied his horses to the rail and walked over toward Joel.

"Hi, dad. How are you?"

"Fine, son. What are you doing here?"

"A lot of things. Mostly to make amends to everyone. I have been doing a lot of thinking these past few weeks. Dad, Margo's death really hit me hard. Harder than I think it hurt everyone else in the family. I shut down and shut everyone out. I went and built that cabin far enough from everyone who could touch me." He stopped when he saw Joel grinning. "What?"

"You met Loren."

"Yes. We sort of rescued each other. She lost her trail around the valley and ended up down inside it. She knew the danger, but couldn't do anything about it because she was lost and trapped. I had seen her campfire from the cabin and went to investigate. My horse saw a snake and threw me. Evidently it wandered into her camp and she found it the next morning with her horses. She came and found me, patched me up and then I helped her find the trail back out of the valley and on her way. She opened my eyes to a lot of things, dad. I think I'm in love with her. She expressed her views of staying secluded in the valley cabin. It was no go. She wanted to be around people, shopping and other stuff.

I almost gave up on her. She found a job in her father's company and I guess is doing well. I haven't heard from her for a couple of weeks. I thought this trip might be an eye opener to me and I can see her again, too. Can I stay here with you for awhile?"

"Of course, son. Mom has been asking if I had heard from you. Let's get your horses put away. Looks like ole Ranger knows your horses."

Andy laughed. "He sure does. He challenged my horse to a race and lost to a water crossing. He refused to cross into the water and Loren ended up in the water after being thrown over his head. It was a funny sight. Very hard not to laugh at her, but Ranger was. He is an extraordinary horse."

"Yes. She wants to buy him."

Together they put the horses in a barn stall. Ranger came in from the back and hung his head over the boards to nose his new buddy. Andy rubbed his nose and then followed his dad out of the barn and toward the house.

After a cheerful greeting from his mother, they sat down to a nice meal. Andy bowed his head as his dad said the table grace. His insides tightened to emotions that he hadn't felt for a very long time. At the end of the meal, Andy called Margo's parents to find out if he could come by and see them. Everything seemed to be working out for good. Joel loaned him his old station wagon for his driving. Andy's mother prepared the guest room for him. Andy went into the bedroom and got ready for bed. A nice hot shower felt good to some of his aching muscles. He returned to the living room where he joined his parents in their evening devotions before everyone went to bed. It felt good to be home again.

After the horses were taken care of the next morning, Andy changed into good clothes in preparation to go to the city.

He had called Grayson Electronics and had an appointment with Mr. Grayson and the production manager just before noon. Looking in the mirror, he wrestled with the tie. It had been too long since he had tied one. He gave up and went to find his mom.

"Mom, I need you."

She turned from the sink and grinned at him. She wiped her hands off the dish towel and walked over to her tall handsome son. "You need to wear them more often Andy. Come here." In just a few quick flips, she had the tie knot made. "Now, when you want to take it off, just slide it down far enough to get your head out and leave it tied. That way you can get it back on later."

Andy hugged her. "Don't know how I could have gotten along without you, Mom. I'll see you later this afternoon or call and let you know when I will be home.

Dad is in the barn working on something. Check on him later, will you?"

His mom frowned. He still remembered back when his dad had that heart attack and was supposed to take it easy.

"Sure. Good luck with Margo's parents. I'm sure they will be open minded for you. It has been a long time and time has a way of healing wounds. We love you, son and really are glad that you came home."

# CHAPTER 14

As Andy reached the city limits, he stopped the car on the road shoulder. So many cars! Where was everyone going? He checked the directions to the Grayson offices and then started back onto the highway. He drove slow irritating a lot of faster driving motorists behind him. Once when he got his bearings, he would go the speed limit. Driving the jeep around in small towns and through the country was child's play next to this. At least the old station wagon was a familiar vehicle.

Soon, the big greystone office building was in front of him. The building was very impressive and well designed. Being an architect originally, Andy could appreciate the building's style. He found a place to park and got out of the station wagon. Self-consciously he wiped his hands down the sides of his pants. Taking a big breath, he let it out slowly. Now he was ready to face everyone. Gripping the briefcase with his drawings and the parts, he opened the front door, entering the office lobby. Expecting to see grand expensive decorations on the walls, he was somewhat pleased by the simplicity of the décor. Some of the portraits on the walls were done by local artists and on display for sale. The woman at the main desk looked up at him and smiled.

"Welcome to Grayson Electronics. May I help you?"

"I have an appointment with Mr. Grayson. I am Andrew Camfield."

"Just one minute." she dialed a number on her phone. Looking back up, she smiled again. "Someone will be here in a minute to take you to his office."

"Thank you." Andy walked a little distance from the front desk as another person came forward to talk to the receptionist. He was studying a painting when a young man in a navy blue suit approached him.

"Are you Mr. Camfield?"

"Yes."

"Follow me, sir." They went to the elevator, got on and pushed the button for the top floor.

Once off the elevator, Andy followed the lanky young man. His blonde hair was cut almost in a crew cut. He reminded Andy of a Marine. A door was opened and they entered a large office. The young man stepped aside to allow Andy to enter the room. A set of several windows almost took up the whole back wall of the room. The view from that window was spectacular. Mountains off in the distance could be seen along with the many skyscrapers about the city far below. The tall muscular built man with graying hair came out from behind the desk with his hand out. Andy grasped it in a firm handshake. He then noticed the other man standing off to the side of the desk.

"Mr. Camfield, this is our production manager, Wayne Rogers. You can put your briefcase over here on the table and lay out what you want to show us."

"All right." Andy put his case on the table and opened it. He pulled out his drawings and set them off to the side, then set the parts on the other side. He pushed the briefcase out of the way. He assembled the paperwork and corresponding parts together before he turned toward the men to begin his presentation. Andy showed them his new part and how it worked. The production manager, Wayne, brought over one of their newly assembled phones. The rest of the morning was spent showing the various ways it would work and make the assembly process quicker.

At noon, it was apparent that Mr. Grayson was beginning to fidget in his chair. It had been a long meeting. Andy could see both men were either bored or overly tired from such a long presentation. He quickly ended his talk to allow all the information to set in. He didn't usually talk so much. He guessed it was the fact that he had lived too long in solitude there in the mountains. He needed to get out more.

Unbeknown to Andy, Loren was in another part of the building preparing to join her father for lunch. She was in the ladies dressing room removing her coveralls. She grimaced at her face in the mirror. She needed a complete makeover. As quickly as possible, she combed through her hair and returned it to the pony tail. Glancing down at her stonewashed jeans and plaid short sleeve blouse, she declared herself ready for lunch. She was definitely underdressed for her father in his suit, but it was the best she could do. Taking a deep breath and letting it out slowly, she left the assembly work area to head to the main office.

Back in Mr. Grayson's office, Andy stopped talking and as he did, he heard a knock on the door. Mr. Grayson stood up and went to the door. Andy almost didn't recognize Loren as she didn't him. Seeing a stranger in the office, Loren almost had to be pulled into the room.

"Mr. Camfield, I want you to meet my working daughter, Loren."

Andy stepped away from the table and slowly approached father and daughter. In a second, they recognized each other. Loren's right hand flew to her face as she turned red. Andy smiled slowly and held out his hand in greeting.

"Good afternoon, Miss Grayson."

"Andy?" surprise lit up her face. Andy grinned at her and finally released her hand.

Mr. Grayson looked at the two. They had met before, but where?

Loren turned her head and looked up at her father. She gave him a weak smile.

"Uh, dad, this is the Andy I was telling you about who helped me out of that valley. We became friends during my journey."

"Well, that is interesting. Why don't you join us for lunch. I'll have Wayne, here, to tell your boss you will be late getting back from lunch."

"All right." What a surprise to see Andy here! Did he know her father?

"Loren, Andrew has developed a new micro chip for the phone we are building. He was showing us how it worked. It will make the assembly a lot quicker. After lunch we will take it downstairs and show Troy and you how it works."

Outside, the limo was waiting. Everyone climbed inside for a ride to a well known restaurant. Loren smiled at Andy and secretly wondered what had been going on in his life since she left him. He made a striking figure all dressed in a suit and tie. His tie matched the blue of his eyes. So handsome! She was slightly uncomfortable in her working clothes sitting next to him.

"How long are you going to be in town, Andrew?"

"I am staying with my parents for a couple of days. I have some unfinished business to straighten up before going home."

"Loren tells me you have a cabin built in the mountains on the edge of that valley she got lost in. That is fairly primitive isn't it?"

"I have a generator and an electrical line stretched from the closest power pole for electricity. It's not too primitive, although I don't have indoor plumbing."

"Andy, who is taking care of your animals?" asked Loren. Concerned about the cow that she knew needed to be milked every day.

"I moved everyone down to Waverly so they could be looked after properly. So, you found your place in your father's business?"

"Yes. I found out that I like working with my hands, so I am in the assembly department. Actually, I will probably be using your chip in the parts that I put together."

"Good. Maybe the two of us can go somewhere and get caught up on everything that has been going on since you left the valley."

Loren nodded. She so wanted to be with Andy again. She could almost tell that he had done some of his restitutions with family members. She was glad that he had started to heal his old wounds.

With the meal at the fancy restaurant over, Andy left them at the front door of the office building. He told Loren he would call her soon. Glancing at his watch, he noted it was time to try to find Margo's parent's home. He climbed into the old station wagon and began his trek across town.

Jesse and Janet were somewhat cool toward Andy as they sat with him in their living room. Andy felt uncomfortable, but started at the beginning when he first found out about the accident. They had a fight and she had gone off angry and crying. Andy had tried to stop her from driving on the wet snowy pavement that night, but she wouldn't listen. She wanted to get away and be alone. Andy told them that he couldn't even remember what the argument was about. A wrong judgment turn of the wheel on an icy bridge spun the car out of control. The only consolation the family received was that she had died instantly. The car was totaled with pieces wrapped around the large tree on the opposite side of the bridge railing. It was fortunate that there was still some daylight to prevent other cars from crashing into the mangled car parts strewn across the road. Andy told them how much he had loved her and had that night asked her to marry him. He didn't tell them that she had told him she was seeing someone else on the side. That part of the story would have devastated them. Filled with compassion, he let tears slip down his cheeks. They felt his sorrow and struggled to forgive him. Andy wiped back the tears and then told them about Loren and her visit to him. He told of her faith in God and it had changed her life.

After thinking long and hard on this concept, he, too, chose to return to his belief in God. Through much prayer he had chosen to make restitution with them and his parents.

Jesse and Janet embraced Andy both wanting very much to mend the strife that had grown between them. Andy left them with a spring in his step and with the urge to sing at the top of his voice. Once back out on the highway, he did just that, although he kept his car windows rolled up. No sense in scaring other motorists off the road!

When he reached home, a wonderful smell of home cooking reached his nose. It felt good to eat someone else's cooking after cooking for himself. His mom looked up from the kitchen counter. She was almost up to her elbows in flour. A large ball of dough sat in the middle of the counter surrounded with flour. A rolling pin sat on one side of the dough. In a bowl was apples all sliced and seasoned with cinnamon and sugar. Andy's taste buds started to water. It had been ages since he had had a homemade apple pie.

"Mom, you are the best." Andy, like he had done when he was a kid, fished out an apple wedge from the bowl.

"Sit down and tell me all about your day." She grabbed a cold drink from the refrigerator leaving white fingerprints on the handle of the refrigerator. She took one for herself and pulled out a chair. Together they talked. Andy told her all about his meeting at Grayson's and with Jesse and Janet. He also told her about Loren and meeting her at her father's office.

"I'm so glad you have healed that old wound of yours. I'm sure they were glad you came by and told them about how you felt and what Margo was really doing."

"Uh, no, Mom. I did not tell them about her seeing the other man. It would have broken their hearts. They thought I was the only one and would soon marry Margo. I have almost accomplished what I have set out to do here."

"What else is there, Andy?"

Andy grinned at her mischievously. "To get fat on your cooking before I leave."

Bessie laughed as she stood up to go back to her pie making. "It won't take long for that to happen. You are welcome to stay as long as you want. Will Mr. Grayson contact you again about your computer chip?"

"I'm sure he will. I'm going to bring Loren here to meet you. Saturday is coming and I'm sure she will be off work. I know Ranger will want to see her again."

"Yes, and she promised to come back out and tell your father all about her trip. She wants to buy Ranger. Dad is not really sure he wants to sell him."

"She loves that horse. The stories she told me about how he protected her by fighting off motorcycle riders when she stopped to visit that revival preacher was enough to want him. He is water shy and that is his only fault I know of. Maybe I'd better go and help dad in the barn."

"He had some new people out today to take riding lessons. He was considering using Ranger."

"He would be great with beginners. See you later, Mom."

Andy found Joel brushing down one of his stable horses.

The horse pricked up its ears when Andy entered the barn. Andy's horse saw him and nickered. Not to be outdone by the others, Ranger nickered too. Andy went to the barrel where Joel kept the horse treats and grabbed a handful. Each horse received their share. Even Brownie ambled up from the back of his stall to get some. He, too, remembered the days on the trail when at the end of the day he received a treat. Joel looked up at his son across the horse's back.

"Grab a brush, son. Your mom probably has dinner about ready."

"Not just yet, dad. She's up to her elbows in flour. There is going to be a big juicy apple pie for dessert."

"I don't know how I'm going to survive all the days you are here, son. She is going to be baking and cooking all of your favorite dishes. I'll be as fat as a pig if she keeps that up while you are here. How many days are you going to be here, so I will know how many days to work off all that weight you are going to help me gain."

Andy laughed and looked at his dad's lanky form. He hadn't really gained much weight since Andy was just a little kid. "Dad, you have always been skinny."

He began stroking the horse with the brush. As he was brushing, he began to relax. Brushing a horse was therapeutic. Even brushing a dog or cat gave a person the same reaction. His dad cleaned out the horse's hooves, then led it to its stall. Andy's horse and Ranger both tried to beg for another treat. Their grain was soon emptied into their feed buckets and hay piled in the corner of their stalls. Andy rubbed each horse's head before sneaking them another treat from the barrel. His thoughts were already on riding again with Loren. Would she come out and ride with him on Saturday? He had promised to meet with her soon so they could catch up on what has been going on between them since she left him several weeks ago. The need to see her was strong. He wondered if she felt the same way after seeing him today.

He walked back in the house with his dad and went to his room to get ready for dinner.

They had so much to talk about since Andy had left several years ago. They talked about their Church family and what had been going on around the city. All the more, Andy wanted to return to his solitude at the cabin. People and friends were okay, but there was just something about being alone with Mother Nature and the animals.

He told his parents about Loren's visit and the changes she had made in his life.

They had enjoyed each other's company, but he expressed his feelings about her not finding living like that attractive enough to stay full time. She had different wants and wishes. True, he was sure he loved her, but was it enough to move closer to the city to please her? The parents expressed their wisdom to their son in hopes that he would find the answer he was seeking.

They urged him to seek out God's Word and find his place with God as the head of his life. Andy accepted the wisdom of his parents and took it to bed with him later that night. In the quietness of his room, he felt the closeness of God. Peace settled upon him as he turned off his light and laid down for the night.

Even though he didn't drift immediately off to sleep, he thought of Loren. Would she accept him as a husband or even a boy friend? He had seen her struggles to accept her, seemingly new found faith in God. He was struggling with that, himself. With what he made off his new microchip software and parts, he could easily support Loren in the life-style she deserved. He wasn't sure about himself, though. He had become accustomed to being alone and in the quietness of his mountain home. High society parties were not anywhere near what he wanted in his life. Angrily he punched the soft pillow back under his head, then rolled over on his side. There would be no sleep for him this night if he couldn't forget everything and let his mind settle. As the room seemed to darken from the night, he relaxed and was soon asleep.

# CHAPTER 15

Loren had just finished an upsetting confrontation with Jeremy. He had come to the house unannounced. His manner was a little rough and his breath smelled of whisky. Loren's parents were cordial to him and invited him into their home. He tried to be charming like he always was, but his mind was fogged by all the alcohol he had drank before coming. He thought several drinks would give him the courage to face her. Now, she was giving him the cold shoulder after all they had done together before she went on that ridiculous horseback trip. Jeremy had met with that other woman from the racetrack and had a few weeks of good times. She was an expensive woman; too expensive for his taste. She had thought he had lots of money, but found out he wasn't prone to spending it; at least on her. He wasn't about to spend his money on an unfruitful fling. Loren presented a challenge to his ego and he wanted her. He hadn't even been able to kiss her, let alone touch her. She still remained the 'ice princess' to him and his friends. He hadn't seen her at any of the parties, but then again, she hadn't been home very long. Now, she was working at her dad's plant like a common person. Loren was trying to be nice, but it was hard with her parents right there, especially her mother. Paula wanted Jeremy to be liked for he was from her favorite friend's society group. She saw how Loren was treating him by giving him the cold shoulder. Through all her suggestions, nothing seemed to work.

Jeremy wanted to take her out to the track that Saturday, but she refused.

"I think I will go ride my horse Saturday. I appreciate your offer, Jeremy, but I'm not interested in the horse racing any longer. Maybe we will see each other again at someone's party later this month. Good bye."

And that had been it. He was shown to the door and he went down the walk to his car in the driveway. He would have to get a party going soon, get her there and maybe spike her drink to get her drunk. Then he could have her the way he really wanted her. With a grin of pleasure, just thinking about it, he revved up is engine and took off. Reaching under the seat, he pulled out a bottle and took a long swig. Tomorrow was another day. Then, we would see what would transpire.

The telephone rang and Loren went to answer it. Andy's voice greeted her. She smiled and sat down on the chair beside the phone.

"Andy! What a welcomed surprise. How are you doing?"

"Wonderful. Do you have plans for Saturday morning?"

"No, I don't."

"How about coming out to the stable where you have Ranger and let's go for a ride."

"Oh I would really like that. I'll bet the old boy misses me. He'll probably buck me off and pretend he stepped into water."

Andy laughed with her. "No, he won't. What time can you come?"

"Do you know where the stable is?"

"Yes. How about nine o'clock. We can pack a picnic lunch and ride back to a lake that is behind the stable property."

"That sounds wonderful. See you then. Oh, I think dad will be calling you soon about that new part and when we can start production. It really works great."

"I'm glad. I am working on other drawings for different electronic equipment and I would like to show them to your father sometime."

"I'll tell him."

They talked for awhile longer, then she hung up. She walked across the room as in a dream. She was truly in love. Paula noticed her daughter as she hung up the phone after listening into the conversation. She couldn't have been talking to Jeremy, because he had just left. Her softened tone was for someone else. The plans for getting her and Jeremy together would have to be gotten underway. The money in his family along with what Grayson made, would make her a lot more wealthy and a tad higher in society. Only thinking of herself, she began plotting out her strategy.

The next several days, Loren worked hard at her job. The other workers found her quite charming and honest. She displayed her Christian values and openly invited anyone willing to join her in prayer for table grace or others for loved ones and sick people. Her father noticed the changes around the assembly department. The workers were not grumbling or complaining any longer.

They were working together as a team; what they were supposed to do in the first place.

Gray was pleased with this turn of events. He only wished it could have happened sooner, but he knew it wouldn't have, because Loren hadn't been there or had been a Christian. He liked this Andy who was making his company more profitable and he felt that he might be in love with Loren, too. Only time would tell. If he could keep Paula from interfering with sticking Jeremy into their lives. He couldn't figure out his wife. She seemed prone on getting them together. Loren and Jeremy had nothing in common. They would not make a good married couple. Shaking his head in confusion, Gray turned back to his desk and went back to work. Time was the answer right now.

Andy's new part was making production quicker and the prototypes were ready for full production. Mr. Grayson contracted a computer company to begin production of the part. Andy was brought in once more to sign a contract to allow the production to take place. Things were moving forward.

# CHAPTER 16

Saturday came with a beautiful warm day in the early fall weather. The trees were just beginning to change color. Andy had his horse in the barn alleyway getting it brushed and ready to saddle. Loren arrived and fairly hopped out of her car. She could hardly wait for this day to come. She grabbed the bag of apples from the passenger seat and closed her car door. She watched a couple of young boys and girls at the corral on horses. Joel was there showing them how to ride. She stood there for a short time, then went toward the barn. As she reached the door, she saw Andy with his horse. Her eyes widened in surprise. His horse? How had he gotten there? She didn't see any horse trailer in the yard. Slowly she advanced toward him. He looked up from tightening the saddle.

"Hey, there, Loren. Ready to ride?"

"I… that is your horse."

"Yep. Rode him all the way here from the valley. I even brought my own pack horse."

"Why would you do that when…." She laughed, tongue-tied by the strange turn of events. Why had he ridden a horse all the way there with no other transportation to drive to the city. She had seen the old station wagon over by the house, but surely he…

"Looks like I have some explaining to do. Go get your horse and we will talk while we ride."

"Okay."

She went to Ranger's stall. He nickered and shoved his head against her chest.

He was so glad to see her! She even brought apples! Yum! She gave him an apple, then went to Brownie and gave him one too. Taking a lead rope from the hanger beside the stall, she fastened it onto Ranger's halter, then opened his stall door. As she led him out, he rubbed his head against her shoulder. It was so good to see her again!

"You silly horse. I hope you remember your manners and let me ride you. I don't think Andy will lead you towards any water traps."

She fastened his lead to a large ring near the tack room door. She brushed him off, then went to find her gear. Andy's mother brought out the picnic basket made to hang onto the saddle horn. In just a short time, both were mounted and reining their mounts toward a rutted road that led to a lake. Andy began telling her all that transpired with his fiancé's parents. Loren was glad that everything was working out for him. She was curious about the valley and the other animals. He had told her someone was taking care of them, but didn't tell her about the new farmhouse with property that he had purchased.

Loren told him about her job and the workers sort of looking up to her for spiritual help. She told him about Jeremy coming back and trying to get her to go out with him to the racetrack.

"What did you tell him?"

"I told him I was no longer interested in the races. He didn't seem to take 'no' for an answer. Mother likes him and father does, sort of. I think they want me to date him."

"And?"

"Andy, I do not feel part of that crowd any longer. The journey I took and being with you has changed me. I am seeking spiritual things now and reading my Bible has helped me tremendously. I would like to find a small church where I can feel comfortable and learn more about Jesus."

"How about going with us tomorrow? We attend a small country church not far from the stable. You already know my parents. Mom can make the best apple pie."

"Ummm. I love apple pie. Really? Home made?"

"Yep. There might be some in this picnic basket along with the fried chicken she made for us."

"Now, I am getting hungry. How much farther is this lake?"

Andy laughed as he glanced at his watch. "It is only ten-thirty in the morning. We won't eat until noon or close to it. The lake is only a half mile ride, but the scenery is beautiful around this area. Fall is here and the trees are changing into their beautiful colors. We can ride for awhile until you really get hungry. I won't mention what else mom put in here."

"You are plain mean, Andy. I never told dad or mom that I have milked a cow. They would be astonished. I'm supposed to be a city girl."

"You still are, with country interests. Your father's company is going to produce my computer chips. I signed the contract the other day. You will probably be seeing a lot more of me here in the city."

"That will be nice. I will probably need a friend once Mom gets in her head to think Jeremy is the man for me."

"Is that the guy that took you to the horse races?"

"Yes. At first, it was exciting. When I found the Bible in the Ladies Lounge, I started reading the story of Jesus with the 100 sheep. The excitement of the racetrack disappeared. That was when I began planning my horseback trip."

Loren was about to continue talking when she saw the lake with all its splendor with the fall colored trees around it. Bright reds, oranges and some yellow hickory trees were dotted across the landscape. Sunlight shone through giving off sunbeams through the trees. Ranger had automatically stopped. Andy reined his horse to a stop also.

This spot would make a nice place to build a home. Every morning would be wonderful to see the changes in the landscape. Andy's view from his new farmhouse was nice, too, but not as great as this. Andy stole a glance over at Loren.

"I've only one word for this. Wow! Wouldn't this make a fantastic spot to build a house? Even the valley can't compare with this."

"Andy, it is wonderful. Who owns this property?"

"Not really sure. Dad would know. He leases it to do trail rides with his students. Is it time to eat yet?"

Loren laughed. "No, silly. It is only about ten minutes later than when you asked me the first time.

Maybe we can ride around the lake and see what it looks like over there."

"Okay."

The ride around the large lake took a long time to accomplish. They more or less had to make their own trail. Some of the smaller animal trails were not wide enough to allow safe passage for horses. When they reached what seemed to be a impassable spot, they turned around and returned another way. There, they found an easier trail that even looked like the one Andy's dad used in his trail rides. Going was a lot faster and they soon were back at their starting point just in time for the lunch hour.

The horses were staked out and a blanket was spread on the ground under a nice shady tree facing the lake.

The two of them talked about various subjects just to get to know each other better. Andy knew then for sure that he was in love with Loren. She was really different being brought up in high society, but deep down, she was honest and sincere. She didn't strut her airs like rich women did. When he asked her a question, she was straight forward in answering him. Once more, he ventured to ask her if she could live in the country, but maybe near shopping. Loren gave him a slightly hesitant yes. She, too, was beginning to love this man. If he had mended all his hang-ups, then she could adjust her lifestyle. Her journey of faith had helped her with that. She no longer required people to wait hand and foot on her. She could cook some and she could probably figure out how to keep house. Shopping in the grocery store had been fun for her. Yes, she could live in the country. After all, she did know how to milk a cow!

With lunch over, they tightened up their saddles and prepared to head back home.

Joel met them at the barn. He had just finished a riding class and was putting the last horse in its stall. Andy had yet to tell Loren that Joel was his father.

Andy dismounted and looped the reins over the hitching post. Now would be a good time to introduce Loren to his father. Loren was down beside Ranger and slipping the saddle loose. She waved at Joel as he started over toward them. He had fastened the last horse in its stall and was now coming to help them with their horses.

"Dad, I want you to meet Loren Grayson."

"Oh, I know Loren."

"Yes, but she doesn't know that you are my father."

Loren looked at both of them. "Well, we finally meet officially. I guess your mom is responsible for that wonderful tasting fried chicken?"

"Yep" Andy and Joel said in unison. "Let's get these horses put away and come into the house for some iced lemonade."

"That sounds like a wonderful idea."

Once in the house, a cool breeze from the air conditioner greeted them. They really hadn't realized how hot it had been outside. This was a pleasant change. Bessie greeted them as they entered the kitchen. Already tall frosted glasses of lemonade sat on the table. Everyone sat down to drink and to get acquainted. Not really needing or wanting to go home, Loren agreed to spend the evening with them for dinner. Andy walked her back to her car at the close of the evening. He would pick her up for church the next morning. Putting his hands on her shoulders, he looked into her eyes. The love for her threatened to come out. She might not be ready to declare her love for him, if she did love him. Andy would be patient. He would be in the city for another week planning his computer component with Grayson Electronics. He had his proposal to marriage all planned out. He was sure she would agree with that plan. He grinned. Loren cocked her head in question. "What are you cooking up? You look like the cat who just swallowed the canary."

"Well, I have a secret, but I can't tell you right now. I will be around for another week working with your father's company and another contractor with my computer chip. I plan on seeing you quite frequently."

Loren smiled and moved her hands up around his neck. Her fingers played with the long hair around his shirt collar. Andy slowly pulled her into his arms. Their faces were now inches apart. Loren's breathing became ragged. She just knew he would kiss her in seconds. Andy moved his hands to cup her face. They say the eyes are the mirror to the soul. He could see the love there. His heart leaped for joy. Maybe his plan would work after all! He saw her eyes slowly close as he bent to press his lips to hers. He heard a moan, not really knowing if it was him or her. His lips devoured hers in the sweetness of the moment. A faint taste of the chocolate cake was there as he touched his tongue to hers. Not wishing to get too intimate he eased back and showered her face with butterfly soft kisses. Loren had just started to melt against him when he had pulled back. Inwardly she was happy. She felt safe and comfortable in his arms. He was truly a gentleman.

The family had talked about spiritual things and were definitely Christians. Tomorrow they would all attend Church and show Loren the true Christian fellowship with other believers. She hadn't been to any Church other than the ones her parents had taken her to when she was little. They were all the big fancy churches that hardly ever mentioned Jesus Christ. She looked at Andy as he pulled away but kept his hands on her shoulders. He let go and they walked to her car. He held the door open for her.

"We will see you in the morning. I'll pick you up about nine o'clock. We can attend the Bible Study classes and then the morning service. Mom has a beef roast she is fixing for our dinner tomorrow. You can come back for lunch after Church."

"That sounds good, Andy. Thank you for the wonderful day. Your parents are great. I'm glad you have worked out your hang-ups."

"I still have a few, but the big ones are over and settled. Drive carefully, Loren."

The drive home was almost like driving in a dream. She really loved Andy. She could tell that he cared for her, too. They really didn't know each other very well, but with the time they would have together there in the city, that would change. She could change to live in the country, but within driving distance of a fairly large town. She thought of Waverly and its size. There had been large stores, the hotel with its wonderful steak dinners and the grocery where she had gotten her supplies for her return trip home. The cabin in the valley, could be a weekend hide-a-way for them. They could ride the horses from Waverly to there in a couple of days. She remembered that Andy had a jeep. She just vaguely remember a trip she took as a young teenager in a jeep through the woods and eventually gotten stuck in the mud. She chuckled. They had had so much fun trying to get out of there! Her dad had banned the boy from the house for a week and made her stay around the house and pool. Wow! What dreadful punishment!

As she turned the last corner onto her street, she saw all the cars parked along the curb.

# CHAPTER 17

The house was all lit up showing signs of a large party in progress. Loren could hear music as she pulled into the driveway. Had her parents planned a party and forgot to tell her? She put her car in the garage and entered the house through the servant's entrance off the kitchen. Sally and the other maids were busy filling trays of horsdoeuvres.

"What is going on?" she asked.

"Your mother decided at the last minute to throw a party to celebrate your coming home. No one knew where you were to let you know to come home."

"They knew I went horseback riding this morning. I didn't know that I was supposed to come home soon after."

"Well, you'd better hurry and change clothes, miss. I'll send someone up to help you dress. It seems like it is sort of a formal affair."

"Thank you. I would much rather hide in my room."

The servants chuckled with her. They knew she had changed for the better and were willing to help any way they could.

Loren crept around the corner into the hallway near the back stairway. She could hear the laughter and clink of glass from the main dining area. As she reached the lower stair, she caught a glimpse of Jeremy passing the doorway. He hadn't seen her. Quickly she fled up the stairs and to her room.

Janet, one of the upstairs maids, came rushing over to her side. Loren patted Janet's arm and led the way into her room. Janet went to the large walk in closet and began pushing the various dresses aside in search of the perfect one. Loren had shed her smelly riding clothes and was heading for the bathroom for a hot shower.

"Janet, could you do my hair? There is a hairdryer in that bottom drawer of the dresser. I'll be out in a sec."

When some of the guests heard Loren's heels on the stairs, they turned to watch her come down. Dressed in a street length pale blue gown, she looked ravishing. Even her mother looked awed and pleased. With a hidden smile of satisfaction, she walked over to greet her daughter. Part one of her plan was working. Loren was here. The rest was up to Jeremy.

"Loren, dear, I'm so glad you could make it. We were worried about you."

"Mother, I told you I was going riding this morning. You said nothing about a party tonight or I would have cut my visit short."

"Where were you?"

"I met Andy's parents and they invited me to stay for dinner. They are wonderful people."

"Yes, well, you are here now. Jeremy is here somewhere. You have only seen him once since you returned."

Loren looked into the room recognizing a lot of her high society friends. They all greeted her in a friendly manner, then went back to their gossiping with the people around them. Jeremy came over and took her arm leading her over to a love seat near the patio door. He had his speech all prepared and the mickey in a vial ready to doctor her drink.

Her mother had given him liberties to do what he wanted with her to get her to marry him. His hands were itching to rip off her clothes and have his way with her. The only way he could manage that would be to get her drunk and unable to respond with resistance.

As they sat down, he snagged a couple of drinks off the tray one of the waiters were passing around. Loren shook her head and refused it. "You know that I don't drink, Jeremy."

"You used to. I'll get you a coke." He left her sitting there and went toward the kitchen. One of the maids handed him the coke in a frosty glass. He poured the mickey into it and stirred the glass around with the ice cubes to mix it. Nervously he carried it back to the sofa and handed it to her. He took his drink from the table and began drinking. Hoping that it would give him the courage to carry out his and her mother's plan. If all went well, she would be drugged enough to be taken across the border and married in one of the many chapels. A one night stand in a motel to consummate the marriage and all would be well.

Sally had just placed extra sandwiches on a tray when she heard Mrs. Grayson bragging to one of her friends about what Jeremy was going to do to Loren in the way of drugging her enough to get her to marry him. Sally had made friends with Loren since she had come home from her horseback adventure. They had spent some time alone in her bedroom talking. Loren had told her about Andy and what a wonderful man he was. Andy needed to be there right now! Sally went to the telephone in the kitchen and thumbed furiously through the yellow pages. She soon found the advertisement for Joel's stable. With shaking fingers, she punched in the number. Hopefully she would not be too late. After a couple of rings, Andy answered. Sally told him what was happening and going to happen if he didn't come soon to help.

Andy hung up the phone. Quickly he slid into his shoes and ran out the door. It would take him twenty minutes to get to her home if the traffic was not too heavy. Prayer was needed and would need to be answered quick. Unfortunately there were no shortcuts to Loren's home. He drove as fast as he dared on the busy roads going into the city and then into the housing development.

Loren felt funny. Everything and the people around the room began to look fuzzy and out of focus. Her arms and legs felt like lead. She didn't even try to describe how her head felt! She was sleepy and she couldn't get her arms and legs to move. Jeremy helped her to stand and she leaned heavily on him. Paula held the front door open for him to help her through it. She handed him a roll of bills and sent him on their way. Jeremy put her into the car and fairly jumped into the driver's seat. The top was down and the evening was still young. He didn't want to wait to get married. He wanted her now! Shifting gears, he drove his car out of the development and headed for a nearby park. There in the grass alongside the lake would be perfect! No one visited the park at this late hour. It was also badly lighted. Down by the lake he drove around the winding road. As he careened around the corner, he almost collided with an old station wagon going the opposite direction. He glanced over at Loren whose head was back on the seat and out like a light. He had wanted her somewhat awake to experience his love making, but he would take her any way he could. As he neared the lake, he saw the headlights of a car behind him. Who could that be? He drove around several roads to shake him off, but couldn't. There was no way he could do what he wanted now. Angrily he drove on trying to escape the person following him.

Andy shoved down the gas pedal and pulled his car up beside Jeremy's. He had recognized Loren in the passenger seat of the two seated convertible. Finding a place to turn around, Andy had raced back to gain ground on the sports car. Side by side they now raced along the road beside the park. The darkness of the night in between street lights gave off foggy shadows that made driving difficult. The narrow road was full of curves to avoid the large trees and spoil the beauty of the park. Thankfully the road was a long one. Neither one could shake the other off. A look of determination furrowed in Jeremy's forehead. He was not going to let this jerk keep him from doing what he had planned with Loren.

Andy shoved his foot down on the accelerator. The old car responded with a jump forward. Soon, they were side by side once again. Jerking the wheel to the right, Andy heard the metal meet metal as the old station wagon grappled with the heavier car. One more sharp jerk to the right of the wheel forced Jeremy to run off the road. Bumping along in the thick wet grass, Jeremy's car spun sideways and slid down a hill toward the lake. Andy braked his car up on the road and was out of his car in a flash, running toward the out of control sports car. The car stopped just as it reached the edge of the lake. Its front right wheel sinking into the muddy water on the bank. Stunned, and dazed, Jeremy grasped the door handle and stumbled out. A big hand grabbed his tie jerking him around. A fast uppercut to Jeremy's chin sent him to the ground and knocking him out cold. Andy whirled back around toward the car that was gradually sinking into the lake. He circled the back of the car and splashed into the lake's cold water to reach unconscious Loren. Jerking the car door open, he reached in and tenderly picked her up off the car seat. He had his hands full trying to make it back up the slippery bank. His feet sunk in the mud, almost pulling off his shoes. Loren moaned. Her head hurt. She felt like throwing up. What in the world had she drank? Andy felt her wrenching and set her down. She vomited and then fell limp in his arms.

She didn't know whose arms she was in, but she felt safe. With a huge effort, she opened her eyes. "Andy." She breathed out breathlessly.

Andy wiped her hair from her face. "Loren, are you all right?"

"Where am I? Did Ranger throw me off again in the water?"

"No, darlin' you had a wild ride with Jeremy. I guess that is who he is."

Andy set her down on a nearby picnic table and went back over to where Jeremy was still out cold. He picked up Jeremy's cell phone and called the police.

A cruiser just happened to be in the area and drove over to where they were. Andy told him that Jeremy had drugged Loren and was running off with her. The officer placed handcuffs on Jeremy and hauled him over to his police car and put him into the back. A wrecker was called to come and haul the car from the lake. Loren was not in any condition to tell the officer what had happened. She would make her statement later.

Andy drove her back to her home, but left her in the car.

"Loren, stay in the car. I'll be right back."

Andy went up to the house and rang the doorbell. He was still muddy from the lake, but didn't really care. He was upset. Sally happened to answer the door.

"Oh, sir, are you Andy?" Sally began wringing her hands nervously.

"Yes. She is all right. I have her out front in my car. Jeremy is in the police station. Can you get to her room to get some of her things together? I don't want her to stay here. She might still be in danger."

"Yes, sir. Follow me up the back stairs. Her step mom and Jeremy put the scheme together. He was to take her across the border and marry her."

"That will never happen. What about Mr. Grayson? Was he in on this?"

"Oh, no, sir. The misses planned the whole thing. She didn't like the change in Loren and wanted to win her back to her ways. If Mr. Grayson knew, he would probably kick the misses out on her rump."

Andy chuckled. They had reached the top of the stairs. Sally led the way to Loren's room.

Once inside, he told her to gather up the necessary clothes she would need to attend Church and to wear to work and ride a horse in. Soon, Sally had everything that was needed. She spotted the Bible on the bedside stand. She would want that, too.

Andy hefted the bag and followed Sally back down the stairs. She led him to the servant's entrance behind the garage.

"Here is the way out, sir. Please tell her we will be praying for her safety. Please let us know how she is doing. Here, call this number. It will only ring in the kitchen."

She wrote out a number and handed it to Andy.

"God bless you, Sally. Thanks for taking the initiative to call me. Here's my card. You can reach me at Joel's stable. He is my father. Thanks again. I'll talk to Mr. Grayson later about this in private. See you later."

Andy left with the bag and hurried back to the car. He drove back home. Loren could stay in the rental cabin behind the house. She would be safe there. He looked at her as he drove with the car windows down. Fresh night air rushed through the old station wagon. Andy could hear the rattle of the torn fender where he had hit Jeremy.

One more bump and scratch was nothing new for the old car. He could fix it Monday.

Loren sighed and opened her eyes. She felt the cool wind blowing across her face. She thought for a moment that she was back in the woods on her ride. The car went over a small bump and she came fully awake.

Looking over to the driver, she saw Andy looking intently at the road ahead. Some late night traffic was building on the main highway leading out of town.

Carefully Andy maneuvered the car around to the slow lane. He glanced then over at Loren. Finding her eyes on him, he smiled.

"So you decided to wake up?"

"Oh, Andy, what in the world happened to me? I remember being at home and a party was going on. Jeremy was there with me and he gave me a drink. I started to feel funny. After that, I don't know. I must have gone to sleep. Do you know anything?"

"Not personally. Sally called me. She was really concerned about your safety. Jeremy could have really hurt you had I not come along when I did."

"I'm so glad that you did. I didn't even know Mom had planned a party for me. She must have planned it and forgot to tell me. Oh, where are we going? It's late. I really need to go home and to bed."

"You are not going back home until I have it out with your parents. Dad has a guest cabin behind the house where you can stay. We will still go to church tomorrow and then figure out what to do next."

They rode the rest of the way in silence. Loren put her head back against the seat and tried to calm down. Nervously she touched her muddy damp dress.

What *had* Jeremy planned to do to her? In the darkness of the car, her face and neck reddened. She thought back several months over the times she had been with him.

He had tried several times to manhandle her against her will. She grimaced.

She knew that he and a few others called her the 'ice princess'. At least she wasn't a easy mark for men. God had protected her even before she had found Him. Just the thought of God being with her sent shivers down her back. She squeezed her eyes shut to hold back the threatening tears. Her hands shook and she put them in her lap. She was getting cold. Her dress was still wet and muddy and so was Andy. Oh what she would give for a hot shower! Her prayer was answered as Andy pulled into his parent's driveway and drove around to a small cabin. Its lights were on and someone was moving about inside. Andy had called from the car while Loren was sleeping. His mom was busy preparing the bed and making sure the heat was on.

Bessie met them at the door when Andy helped Loren walk inside. She stepped forward and put a comforting arm about Loren's shoulder. In a motherly fashion, she took her back into the bedroom. Like a small child, Loren allowed herself to be undressed. She was still coming out of the drug and not functioning very well on her own. The wet soggy gown was ruined. It was dumped on the floor. Andy put the suitcase on a low table.

"Here's her clothes, Mom. Her maid, Sally fixed a bag for her. I guess you will finish up here? I'll go on up to the house. Dad still awake?"

"Yes. You look like you could use a good scrubbing, too, son. I'll have her fixed up in no time. Run along now. The hot water tank has been turned on. She'll feel a lot better after a nice hot bath."

Andy chuckled. "You make a good mother hen, mom."

Bessie made a shooing gesture at him, then turned to her charge. Loren was practically dead on her feet.

The drug was just beginning to wear off leaving her with a nasty headache. Inside the shower, she turned on the hot water. She yelped as the water was hotter than she was expecting. Grabbing the knobs, she adjusted them to her pleasure. Letting the hot water pour over her, she slowly relaxed before grabbing the soap to lather up good. The mud and lake water was soon washed away. A big fluffy towel was wrapped around her as she stepped out of the shower. Bessie was right there to help her pull on the floor length flannel gown.

"Now, to bed with you, missy. Sit on the chair and I will brush out your hair. It should dry quickly. Oh, Janet packed a hair dryer in your bag. A very thoughtful friend."

"Sally is our cook at our home. We have become friends. Christian friends. She is now a believer."

Bessie beamed with a large smile. "That is wonderful, darlin'." She patted the bench in front of the dresser and Loren obediently sat down facing the mirror. Bessie began brushing her hair, humming as she worked. Loren felt so relaxed. It had been what seemed forever since she had her hair brushed. She thought back to her real mother and all the love that she was given as a child. Tragic to end her life in a bad accident leaving her alone at a young age with her grieving father. Her dad had come home with Paula after a short fling on a business trip. Loren had looked forward to having a new mother who would love and care for her like her real mom. That just did not happen. Paula had not been a mothering kind. Now, she was in the care of Andy's mother.

With her hair dried and brushed until it shone, she was ready for bed. Even her Bible was among her things. Climbing into bed after Bessie left, she stuffed an extra pillow behind her back and sat up to read awhile. Into Psalms she went for comfort scripture. She read the 23rd Psalm again. She put her hand over her mouth to cover a huge yawn. Reluctantly she placed the Bible on the bedside table and turned off the light. Snuggling down into the warm covers, she quickly drifted off to sleep.

# CHAPTER 18

Church with Andy and his parents was a wonderful experience. It was a small church with about one hundred in attendance. The pastor preached a salvation message and several went forward. Loren watched. She had never gone forward, but had already accepted Christ as her personal Savior. Andy grasped her hand as the final words were sung of the invitation hymn. She felt so close to him now. She loved him. Would he declare his love for her as well?

They went back to the house for lunch. Loren went to change into everyday clothes. She wondered what she should do. Andy hadn't talked to her much about what had happened last night. Maybe she should confront him or go home and talk to Sally.

When she returned to the main house, everything was on the table waiting her arrival. Everything smelled so good! Even though she was hungry, her appetite faded as the unanswered questions kept pushing through her mind. She would wait until after the meal to talk to him. How much did his parents know about last night? She found her appetite was now nil. Everything was delicious, but she wasn't hungry. She pushed the food around on her plate, smashing some of the green beans into the mashed potatoes. She wanted answers to her questions first. Andy saw that she was puzzled about something. He thought it was about last night. She would want to know everything.

After the meal was over and Bessie shooed them out of the kitchen, he followed her outside. They sat down on the porch swing. Andy turned sideways to face her.

"Okay, Loren, what is bothering you,?"

"I want to know everything about last night. What can you tell me?"

"I have told you almost everything that I know from Sally. She called me and told me you were in danger. She had overheard your mother talking to Jeremy about getting you drunk, then driving across the border and marrying you. She wanted him in the family and she knew that he liked you. I don't really know why he was taking you to the park, but that is how I was able to catch up with him. He lost control of the car and almost put you in the lake."

"I can't believe that dad went along with that! I thought we were close. I really need to confront them. Will you go with me?"

"Yes, but you are coming back here to stay. I don't trust them. Jeremy might be in jail today, but he will probably be bailed out and will be twice as dangerous. If you are ready to go, we will now."

"Yes."

When they reached the Grayson home, Andy led her around to the servant's entrance. Knocking on the door, soon brought Sally to answer it. She smiled in greeting, but seemed on edge. She motioned for them to enter, then ushered them to the back room, closing the door.

"Oh, Miss, are you all right?"

"I'm fine thanks to you, Sally. We came to straighten things out. Are my parents home?"

"Yes. They had a bad argument last night after everyone left. Your father was fit to be tied. Never has he been so mad at the misses. I don't think he knew anything."

"I was hoping that was the case. I want you to tell me exactly what you heard my mother say and then take me through everything step by step."

Sally motioned for them to sit down. She took a deep breath and breathed out slowly. This might cost her job, but Loren deserved to hear the truth. She told the both of them about hearing the plans for getting her drunk, then hauling her off. The misses knew Loren didn't drink alcohol, but Jeremy could put the Mickey into another drink. The misses had handed Jeremy some money for their 'wedding'. Whatever he wanted to do to her afterwards, would be fine. Sally told them that the Mister, was outraged upon hearing about the plan along with the party. Lowering her voice, she told them that they had even slept in separate bedrooms last night.

Andy rubbed his chin. How would he handle this? Loren really needed to do the talking to both parents, but really maybe her father first.

"Sally, where is Mr. Grayson right now?" asked Andy

"He's in the library. I can take you to him without the misses seeing us."

"Good. Ready to face the lion in his den, Loren?"

"Let's have a word of prayer first." They stood up and held hands with Sally. With heads bowed and eyes closed, they prayed for the right words to be spoken and a good ending for this situation. Squeezing Sally's hand, Loren looked into her eyes.

"We will remember you, Sally. None of this will come out that you told us."

"Thank you, Miss."

Sally led the way across the house toward the library. She left them at the closed library door. Looking at the heavy wooden doors, Loren inwardly shivered. So many times in her childhood, she had dreaded entering those doors. Sally quickly walked off in order to keep out of the inquiry, she needed to be elsewhere. Loren knocked on the door. At the 'come in', they entered.

Mr. Grayson about came out of his chair in surprise. Grabbing the edge of the desk, he regained his balance. The chair spun sideways on its wheels stopping several feet away. He had not expected Andy to appear with Loren. He straightened to his full height and walked around the desk. With his hand outstretched for a handshake, he tried to smile. Andy ignored the hand, not offering his in return. Mr. Grayson dropped his hand.

"Mr. Grayson, your daughter was badly treated here last night. I think you owe her an explanation."

"Well, it really was my wife's idea. How are you involved?"

"I'll tell you later. Please explain last night to Loren. I'm here for moral support." Andy reached for a chair and pulled it over to the desk for Loren to sit down.

Even Loren shied from her father's embrace as he tried to approach her. He would have to re-earn her trust, and be resigned to listen as well as to explain last night's happenings.

"Have a seat and we will discuss this, then I'll have someone go and get Paula."

With everyone seated, Loren started talking, telling her father what she knew of the events leading up to her getting drugged. Her father turned ashen. He didn't know about that. He only knew about Jeremy going to take Loren out for a ride in his car for some air. What was this about him trying to marry Loren?

"Surely you are wrong, Loren. I know you don't care for Jeremy. Why would he want to take you out and……NO! Loren, he didn't! Please tell me he didn't have his way with you!"

"No, dad, but he came close, I think. I was unconscious at the time. Andy told me he saw Jeremy driving toward the park and tried to stop him. Jeremy lost control of the car and almost drove both of us into the lake. Andy rescued me and took me back to his parent's home. I stayed in their guest cabin last night. I can't come back here until it is safe. Jeremy is probably out of jail now and will try again unless something is done."

"Wait. Why is Jeremy in jail?"

"He put his car in the lake so he was charged with reckless driving. I called it in when I stopped to help

Loren before she went into the lake. He lost control of his car and spun around on the wet grass. He didn't correct it until the car stopped on the lake's bank. Like Loren said, he will probably post bail and be out if he is not already out today. I didn't tell the officer about Loren being possibly kidnapped. I'll leave that decision up to all of you. It is not safe for Loren to stay here any longer. She will stay with my parents in their guest cabin behind the main house. I will be going back home after the end of our business. If a restraining order is made out against Jeremy coming here, then she will come back. Those orders usually don't work in all cases. I don't know anything about Jeremy, so I can't tell you how to go about this situation."

"All right. I'll try to get this thing settled. Loren, will you still be coming to work?"

"If you want me to, dad. I rather enjoy working."

"Do you need to hash this out with your mother? I will send her packing, if that will help."

Loren looked over at Andy. What should she do? It was really up to her.

"Let's pray first, then I will go up to her room and talk to her alone. Dad, will you pray with us?"

Mr. Grayson cleared his throat and gave her a slight nod. She reached over and took his hand and Andy's. She bowed her head and prayed for guidance in the next few minutes and for God to give her the needed strength for the encounter she was about to face. Her father was a pussycat compared to the wrath she would face with her mother.

Paula sat in her room trying to relax after the argument with Gray. When she heard the soft knock on her door, she thought he had come to apologize. She got up and ran to the door, flinging it open. Her eyes grew huge in surprise to find Loren standing there. Her mouth moved to speak, but nothing came out. Silently she stepped back allowing Loren to enter. Her hands began to shake, then she pulled herself together ready for another fight.

"Paula, we need to talk. Let's sit down."

Paula looked at Loren. She never called her that. She had been calling her 'Mom'.

They sat down on the chairs in her lounging section of the bedroom facing each other. Loren placed her hands on her lap, then looked Paula in the eye.

"Paula, I really don't know what you were thinking last night when you put me in Jeremy's charge. He has no intention of marrying me. He has been wanting to have his way with me every since I first went out with him. He is a lady's man and would not settle down to one woman, even if it was me. You, see, my life has taken a drastic change since my horseback journey. I found Jesus Christ, Mom. He is real. It is not a religion, but a personal relationship with Him. We can talk to Him, telling Him everything that is going on in our lives. God sent Him to earth to die on the cross for everyone's sins. After three days, He arose from the grave, proving to the world that He can conquer death. He loves, you, Mom."

Paula looked at her stepdaughter. She had heard these same words way back when she was just a young teenager. Getting into the wrong crowd and scrambling to reach it big in high society made her forget all her Bible teachings. She remembered Bible stories from her childhood. They had seemed so fairy tale now, but they didn't back then. The teachers had read them straight from the Holy Bible and it was God's Word. Not in a million years did she think she would ever hear about God again, not now. Her heart told her to accept the Word, but her head wanted to refuse. She had seen the changes in Loren, but wasn't really sure what had caused them. Now she knew. Loren *had* found God. Gray had come back from seeing her at the end of her horseback trip and commented on the change in Loren. Paula had just chalked it up as a change from having a pampered life to having to do everything for herself.

She looked up at Loren. Was she expecting her to do something right then?

She began to feel uncomfortable. Her mind was beginning to shut God out once more. "We, I mean, I need to think. Please leave. There will be plenty of time for me to find God. I'm just in the prime of my life."

Loren slowly shook her head. "People die young, Mom. No one is promised tomorrow. Today is the day of salvation. Let me pray with you."

"No! Just leave me alone." Paula stood up and moved away. Loren also stood and walked toward the door. Maybe she could let her think about it for awhile.

"I'm not staying here. I have moved into a guest house until it is once more safe for me to be here. Jeremy might still be wanting to get to me and I can't let that happen. Dad knows where I will be. Please think about accepting Christ, Mom. I'll be there for you."

"Just get out!" Red-faced with anger, Paula tore at the handkerchief in her hands.

The idea of her speaking that way to her, her own mother!

Back in the library, Loren relayed what had transpired with her mom. Her father agreed that she should find a safe place to stay.

"Have Janet pack some of your clothes and keep in touch. When you come to work Monday, I can give you a phone to try out. It has Andy's new chip in it."

Loren hugged him and followed Andy out the door. Janet did as she was told and went upstairs with Loren. Soon, they were on their way back to the stable. Loren remained silent all the way to the stable and the guest house. Andy kept looking over at her as he drove, hoping she would at least say something.

# CHAPTER 19

A couple more days went swiftly by and no sign of Jeremy. Loren was back into her work and making progress. She loved being in the guest cabin and around Andy's mother. She mothered her almost to the point of spoiling her. Andy visited her during the lunch hour to keep tabs on her. His time there was running out. He still hadn't approached her with his proposal. Everything was going good with his computer chip production. If all plans worked out, he would be ready to saddle up and head back to Waverly, alone.

Sally had just finished cleaning up the dishes from Mrs. Grayson's room when she overheard her on the telephone. Stopping to listen outside the door, she overheard her say, 'Jeremy'. Was she talking to that cad? After the talk she had had with Loren? She must find out what was really being said. Quickly she hurried down the back stairs to the kitchen. Easing up the telephone receiver, she listened to the conversation. Her face paled at what was being planned between the two. She knew that neither one knew where Loren was living, but Jeremy could follow her from work. She must contact Andy at once! Paula knew that one of the servants had helped Loren escape Jeremy's first try for Loren. Now, she had to figure out who.

This final plan must succeed, then she would have to move, also. Once Gray got wind of her part in it, she was a cooked goose. Grabbing a sweater, she hurried down the stairs.

Once in the kitchen, she looked around, scrutinizing everyone there working. All of the maids tried to hide their nervousness. They knew they would be fired instantly if the Misses knew of their part in Loren's protection. Sally was on the telephone calling Andy. Paula hadn't seen her and asked Janet where she was. Janet shrugged her shoulders, then pointed toward the bathroom area. Paula waited, tapping her foot impatiently.

"I'll go get her Madam." offered Janet.

Paula nodded, then began drumming her fingers on the counter while she waited. Janet scurried off toward the bathroom area. That was where the telephone was, too. She tapped Sally on the shoulder just as Sally started to walk away.

"The Misses wants to see you. I think she suspects one of us of helping Loren. Can you keep a straight face? I told her you went to the bathroom."

Sally nodded. "We need to pray hard on this one, Janet. She is a devil herself. She was talking to that Jeremy again. They are cooking up something terrible for Miss Loren."

They reached the kitchen and stood silently before their Misses. Paula looked at each one; her eyes drilling into theirs. When Janet and Sally had entered the kitchen, all of the servants were lined up standing at attention. Paula cleared her throat and began pacing back and forth in front of them.

"Now, I know Loren is my dear stepdaughter, but I have plans for her future and I don't appreciate interference from any of you. You are servants and are required to do as you are told. Jobs are not that easy to find around the city and pay as good as I am paying all of you. Now, in order to keep your present positions, please tell me who informed that outsider friend of Loren's about Jeremy taking her for a ride in his car?"

No one moved. They knew that wasn't what really happened. No one was going to tell them that cad was simply taking her a ride in the park. None of them liked Jeremy.

Paula smiled. Money usually talked. She would offer them a large amount of cash for helping her rat on the guilty person.

"How much would it be worth to tell me what I want to know? Fifty, one hundred, five hundred dollars? For the right information, I could go as high as one thousand dollars."

Several of the servants looked at each other. Loren had built a bond between them in the last several weeks and no amount of money should break it. Loren had told them about Jesus and several had accepted Him. They knew their lives would change, and there would be rough decisions to make along the way. Here was the first one that had come to them. The servants who had not accepted Christ began to get itchy and the feeling of greed come upon them. One servant sort of nodded his head at Paula and she acknowledged it with a slight nod. Sally caught the nod and swiftly looked at the servant.

He was fairly new to the Grayson's and hadn't really fit in with the others. He needed a lot more instruction and training as to the ways of the Grayson household.

Sally made a mental note to gather the others around and tell them not to give out any information within hearing range of the new man. They were all dismissed and went back to their duties. Paula left the room and with a pleased look on her face went to her quarters. Money really could talk. Now, if the right information could be gotten from that servant things could go her way. Slowly, though, she realized that he was a new employee and might not know what she wanted. Oh, well, he would continue trying to infiltrate the rest of the servants to gain their confidence. All in good time. Paula went off to her suite to dress for going out. She was meeting Jeremy at the Club. They had plans to make for their second attempt to get Loren out of her hair.

Sally and the other servants converged on the new servant. In just a few stern words they advised him to stay with them and not pursue the 'blood' money. Even though the amount seemed huge, the rewards and how he would feel afterwards could not compare to the betrayal he would be doing to the daughter of the house.

Paula ordered the chauffer to bring her car around. She took up her purse and left the house. She was taken to another part of the city where Jeremy lived. When she came to the house, there was a car in the driveway. The butler showed her into the living room and was told to wait while he summoned Jeremy. While he was gone, Paula heard giggling coming from the back of the house. Not waiting for the butler to return with Jeremy, she walked that way. There was Jeremy with a woman in his arms. As she watched, she suddenly realized that the planned marriage scheme would not work. He was the womanizer that Loren said he was. How embarrassing for her! No amount of planning could take place now. She was defeated!

Even though she was highly jealous of Loren, she would not subject her to this, this cad! She had been led to believe that Jeremy had true affections for Loren and would cherish her once she was his. He was nothing but a womanizer! Turning on her heel, she quickly exited the house. She resolved right then that she would not do anything else to spoil Loren's happiness. She knew that she had met someone else, but hadn't met him yet. She had heard Gray speak of a young man who had invented a computer chip for his company. Loren had somehow met him on that horseback ride she had taken a couple of weeks ago or was it months? Whatever. Now, she probably needed to talk to the servants once more and straighten everything out. She was changing. How had all that come about? Was it God? Could He be coming into everyone's lives and changing them? When she reached home, she even thanked the driver when she exited the car. He sat there with his mouth open in utter surprise as he watched her walk up to the house. He had not been in on the servant's talk, but knew something was happening for the better around there.

Janet saw her come into the house and walk toward the kitchen. She hurried down to the laundry room to warn them that the Misses had returned. She was just on her way back to her work area when the intercom summoned all the employees to the kitchen.

Once more they stood at attention before a different Paula. Her harsh expression was one of a softer nature. She even made an attempt to smile. She cleared her throat and began her speech.

"Ladies and gentlemen, I want to straighten up my previous tirade. I really don't know why I am telling you all of this, but after leaving here awhile ago, I was fully intent on getting Jeremy to try again at Loren. After seeing him in his environment, I realized I have been wrong. If you can, forgive me and forget what I said earlier, I will make no more trouble for Loren. I have been a jealous woman. I really don't know what has come over me, but I think God has something to do with it. When Loren returned from her trip, she was a changed woman. You all probably noticed the changes. She took upon herself to do things for herself. I think she almost put Sally out of work. She has made a difference in everyone's lives around here and it seems that it is for the better."

Some of the staff laughed. They knew that was true. Loren had been doing things that a grown woman should. Janet didn't have to lay out clothes for her to wear or to clean up after her. Even the cook was relieved of some of the work in the kitchen with Loren helping. The servants listened to Paula speak and could readily tell she was telling the truth. Their prayers were being answered. As Paula quit talking, the servants thanked her and were dismissed to continue their work. Almost in a daze, Paula returned to her rooms. She really didn't know what had transpired. Had she really thanked the servants? Changing out of her good clothes, she dressed in her every day dress. Downstairs in the library, she ventured inside. Slowly she walked over to the big desk where Gray worked when he brought home some paperwork. She ran a finger across the top of the highly polished walnut finish. Her finger stopped midway against a book. A Bible! Was he reading one of those? Only for a moment her mind started to rebel. No! She was going to find out what all this God stuff meant. A few childhood memories surfaced in her mind. She had loved the love stories found in the Old Testament about Esther, Sarah and Ruth. Walking around to the chair, she sat at the desk and placed her hands on the Bible. She felt the smooth leather cover beneath her soft palms. As her hands rubbed over the cover, a bookmark stuck out of the top near the back. Slowly she pulled back the pages to that place. Gray was reading in the New Testament from the Book of John. His marker was at the third chapter. Paula began to read the story of Jesus and Nicodemus. The thirst to know more hit her. On and on she read about Jesus healing the sick and then about his crucifixion. This was what Loren and the others had talked about! Jesus had died on the cross for her! A lone tear escaped from her right eye. Paula slowly brushed it away but not before another one had formed and followed the first down her cheek. How hard she had let her heart get! Slowly she closed the Bible and laid her hands on top.

Bowing her head, she stammered through a prayer half under her breath in total repentance. Both eyes were shedding tears with them dropping onto the cover of the Bible. She now felt the rush of forgiveness engulf her. A smile split her face as she raised her face toward the ceiling in thanksgiving. Her sins were forgiven! She vaguely remembered hearing this story, but paid it no mind. About that time she was seeing a boy in her class and they had started making advances toward a friendship. With her mind off on courting and having him spend money on her, all thoughts of the Bible and Church fled her mind.

From that romantic encounter, to another completely different one, led her further from God. She found herself a teenager on the brink of ruining her life forever. As she grew older and wiser, she realized that high society would be an excellent place to be. With her goal set, she began striving for that particular goal and to snag a wealthy man in the process. That was when she attended a party in the largest house she had ever been in and saw Gray Grayson. What a dashing figure he made! Through several of her acquaintances, she learned that he had recently lost his wife and had a young teenage daughter. A large company owner, rich in his own making and a good catch. Soon, she was flattering him with her wiles and tempting him with her slim and vibrant body. It wasn't long after that party that they soon became a couple. She played it up with the young spoiled daughter and won a place in their lives. The marriage was the top social event of the season. She had made her mark in top society.

# CHAPTER 20

Andy made a quick trip back to Waverly using the old station wagon. He wanted to check on everything and plan for Loren's presence. New furniture had arrived and was ready to move into their spots in the home. Out at the barn, Old Tom snubbed him as he went to milk the cow. He had been without his usual squirt since Andy had left. The man who was in charge, hadn't offered the cat any fresh milk. On some milking trips, the man had actually shooed the cat away. Andy set the milking stool down and brought out the cow. The cat watched, wondering if it had a chance at some milk now that the owner was there. Slowly it made advances toward Andy and stood in its best spot to catch a spray of milk. Andy saw it there and let a squirt fly watching the cat open its mouth and catching the steady stream of warm milk.

He chuckled at the cat, then turned around to continue the milking. The sound of the milk hitting the bottom of the bucket was soothing to the ear.

As Andy worked around the farm, he began missing Loren. She was in his every thought. Even in his sleep, visions of her lovely face was there. He must really declare his love for her. Each day, though, brought a new problem to solve keeping him from returning to the city and Loren. Weeks went by and no word from Loren from her cell phone. Had she forgotten him? He knew she really enjoyed her work, but this silence was getting ridiculous. Maybe she didn't really care that much for him. Now where did that thought come from? He knew she cared for him. Then another thought came to him. Had Jeremy finally gotten to her through her mother? Time was not good for him right now. He *had* to go to her! Back in his office, he prepared the next set of drawings to show Grayson. He packed his overnight bag and went out to the old station wagon. He really needed to get it back to his dad. He had left him with no transportation for… How many weeks? Too many to count.

Once at home, he found his parents getting anxious about him. They had needed to go to the city several times and hadn't been able to reach him on the phone. They hadn't heard from Loren either.

"I'm sorry, dad, mom. I ran up against all kinds of problems at the farm. I hadn't heard from her, either. Listen, I have decided to ask her to marry me. Do you suppose we can have the service in the back lot overlooking the lake? We both loved that spot."

"That's wonderful, son. How about running us into to the city and dropping us off at the grocery."

"I'll drive you to a car rental and I'll get a car and you can have yours back. Are you ready to go?"

Sitting behind the wheel of a shiny black sedan, Andy drove on to Grayson's Electronics. He was ushered into the office and was greeted by Mr. Grayson. Today, he had his suit coat off and sleeves rolled up. Andy felt more at home in his presence this time around.

"What can I do for you today, Andrew?"

"I have some new drawings for you to consider, but I really wanted to know how Loren is. I haven't heard from her."

Mr. Grayson smiled. "She is doing wonderful here at the plant. All of the workers think she is the greatest. Our work level has risen tremendously and everyone seems to be working together as a team. She has even started a prayer chain.

If anyone has a family member sick or themselves, they all gather on their break and pray for them. I really don't understand it. My wife has even accepted Christ and is now more loveable toward me and the servants. God has really taken over around here."

"Maybe God has found a way into everyone's lives here. Loren had opened my eyes to His love for me. I started reading my Bible again and now I feel that I am back on track. You wouldn't believe the hang-ups I had before she showed up at my valley. I am really getting off the subject. Do you suppose I could see her for a short time?"

"Why certainly. Let's take a walk through the assembly section and you can see for yourself the progress of your computer chip. We have almost doubled our sales and everyone seems to be working better. The stress seems to be less in different departments."

Everyone nodded a greeting to the men as they walked through their departments. Some recognized Andy from when he was there the first time to introduce his computer chip. As they approached Loren's section, Andy watched her working side by side with another man. Her face was animated with pleasure of doing her job. Streaks of grease was on her cheeks where she had rubbed them in the process of working with the oiled parts. Andy fell in love with her all over again. She was truly a rich girl brought up in the city, but now not afraid to rub elbows with working people.

Her journey of faith had really changed her. His heart gave a leap when she turned and saw him with her father. The look of love in that look could not be hidden. She loved him! The urge to run to her and throw his arms around her and kiss her thoroughly was held in check. This was not the place. He walked toward her as she came around her work station to meet him. He took her hands in his and devoured her with his eyes. All of the other workers close by watched. They knew him to be the chosen one for Loren. Letting caution to the wind, Andy cupped her chin and lowered his lips to hers. She threw her arms around his neck and leaned into the kiss. She was hungry for him! So much had transpired that had kept them apart.

Voices in the background rose in a cheer as they slowly parted. Loren's face turned red with embarrassment. Andy chuckled and kept holding her hands. Mr. Grayson cleared his throat. He turned to the workers.

"All right, let's get back to work."

"Andy, where have you been? I couldn't reach you on the phone."

"I have moved and changed my phone number. I want to ask you something."

He pulled out the ring box from his pocket and got down on one knee right there in the middle of the assembly department. Still holding one of her hands, he opened the box. "Loren, will you marry me?"

Loren blushed once more. She only saw the love in his eyes to know he truly loved her. She also knew he had come back to God and had taken care of all his old hang-ups that had kept him from God.

"You haven't asked me if I love you."

Andy looked up at her. "Well? Do you? I love you."

Loren nodded. "Yes! I love you."

Andy then slid the ring onto her finger, then stood up. Everyone cheered and clapped. Their boss's daughter had finally found true happiness. Some of them had been praying for her to meet someone who would love and cherish her. Mr. Grayson smiled at them. Who would have thought that someone would propose marriage right there in his plant. He glanced at his watch. Production was ahead of schedule.

"Everyone, in honor of this occasion, I declare an early lunch hour. Report back to your stations at your regular return time. That means you have an almost two hour lunch hour. Spend it wisely. Thank you for your good work."

Loren took Andy's hand and they walked out into the main lobby. She was fairly bouncing with joy. She hadn't felt so happy since winning the horse race with him in the valley. They sat down in the comfortable chairs over in a quiet corner. Andy faced her and took her hands again.

"I have some ideas for the wedding. How about having the wedding there facing the lake? That piece of property behind Mom and Dad's. The trees are still in their fall colors and haven't started to fall off as yet. Afterwards, we can get the horses ready for our ride back to Waverly for our honeymoon."

"That sounds like a good plan. When do you want to do this?"

"As soon as possible. There is bound to be rain coming that will tear the leaves from the trees and spoil the beauty of the spot. How about next week? Will that be enough time to get ready?"

"It should be. We don't need a huge wedding. Let's go tell dad." Grabbing his hand, she pulled him through the plant aisles toward the outside door. Several workers still on their way toward the lunch area, smiled and offered them congratulations. Their prayers had been answered.

Like two children, Loren and Andy almost skipped through the hall toward the main offices. They embraced and kissed in the elevator as they rode up to the top floor where Mr. Grayson had his office. She turned a bright red when the elevator door opened and her father was standing there in the process of going down.

He chuckled and got into the elevator. "All right, you two. How long has this been going on?"

"Since the first floor, I think." The three laughed together. "Are we going to lunch together?"

"I believe so. Did you want a word with me?"

"We are getting married, dad. Do we have your blessings?"

Mr. Grayson beamed with pride. "You certainly do! When?"

"Uh, maybe next week?"

"That's a little soon, don't you think? Women need lots of time to prepare for things like that. Dresses, reception stuff, cake, etc. Oh and invitations.!"

"We plan to have it outside on a piece of property behind my parent's home. It is on a lake and the trees are just beautiful right now. I'm afraid if we wait too much longer, the trees will begin to shed their leaves and it won't look as pretty."

"Okay, kids. We'll see what we can conjure up. The kitchen staff will need to get preparations in order. I am the first person you have told?"

"Yes, daddy. Isn't it wonderful?"

"You seem to be getting a fine young man."

The elevator came to a halt on the ground floor. Slowly the doors opened to the lobby. All three walked off, but two were seemingly walking on clouds above the floor.

A flurry of preparations in the next couple of days whisked them closer to the wedding day. Paula got right into the fray along with all the servants. They were in the preparation stages of preparing some of the food for the outdoor wedding. No invitations were made or sent out. Only the Grayson staff and a few of their closest friends were to be in attendance along with Andy's side of the family.

# CHAPTER 21

Wedding preparations were in the works. Paula went with Loren to pick out her gown. Andy returned to the stables to prepare for the service. His Church would do the ceremony and a local photographer was called in to photograph the location to create a wall hanging to put on one of their home's walls.

Paula looked at the radiant Loren as she posed in a wedding gown. She never in a million years thought she would be in this position. A single tear escaped from her eye. Quickly she brushed it away. Loren was beautiful. Paula had never had a child through any of her male acquaintances. This was a very special occasion for her. In a way, she was glad God had entered everyone's lives at the Grayson residence. She had not fully understood the way of salvation, but her heart was softened to its call. She had told Loren about her decision to accept Christ. Loren had been thrilled and had immediately hugged her. Now she whirled around showing off the full length gown. and called to her.

"Mom! How do I look in this one?"

Mom. She had called her Mom! It had always been Paula. Her heart swelled with happiness. She had been forgiven from all her evil doings. She was a real Mom. Getting up from her chair, she walked over for a closer look at the lovely white laced gown with a short flowing train. Puffy long sleeves would be appropriate for the winter season now approaching. The store clerk placed a laced veil on her head. Paula's fingers nervously straightened the veil out and down the back of the gown. She looked like an angel.

"This one is just perfect for you, Loren." Paula turned toward the sales clerk.

"We'll take it."

Loren lifted the skirts and went off to change back into her street clothes. The clerk followed to help her undress. Paula felt at peace. She had been reading the Bible, too, in secret. She was beginning to feel the love Christ had on her heart. Once more she swiped at a stray tear. She rarely became emotional. Loren came bouncing back into the room and wrapped her arms around Paula. Hugging her, she kissed her on the cheek.

All the bad feelings she had toward Paula were gone. She was now accepted as a mother.

With the gown safely boxed and placed in the limo, they continued to shop. Shoes needed to be bought as well as maybe a going away outfit. Loren laughed when she told Paula they were riding their horses after the reception was over. Paula didn't miss a lick. Then they would buy jeans, shirts and maybe a warm jacket. The day turned into a wonderful day. It was the best that Loren had ever had with her mom. She suspected Paula of gradually changing toward God and rejoiced. So much had happened since she had met Ken there in the city on the street corner. Lives had been changed and some were still in the process of changing. The biggest change she noticed, was that of Paula. Paula had been all for herself. She wouldn't show love for anyone. Being above everyone else was her top concern. After all, she came from high society after a lot of struggling and she intended to stay in high society. Loren didn't know Paula's past and it really was no longer important. She was changing for the better and that was what counted.

As the days flew by, the day of the wedding finally came. Everyone in the Grayson household was in a flurry preparing for the big day. The kitchen crew was preparing the appetizers and a few of the main dishes to be taken out to the stable. Joel was preparing a barbeque meal in the large grill the church had loaned him. Several church members were on hand to help him with the meat. Tables were set up across the back lawn. Andy and a couple others had raked the lot free of manure. Ranger watched from the fenced area near the barn. Something was going on. He had seen the packing gear hauled out again and was cleaned and made ready for a trip. Excitement built up in him. He snorted and began prancing around in the corral. Soon, Brownie and Andy's horse took part in the excitement as they bucked and ran around in the enclosure.

A group came with their musical instruments to play the wedding march and music for the service. All of the guests were beginning to arrive. Most of the food was placed in a clean stall on covered tables. The chairs were already set up back on the lot behind the stables facing the lake. Guests began walking the short distance to the hillside. Andy and the minister were already standing at the place where the lake could be seen in all of its splendor.

The Grayson limo pulled up beside the guest cabin and everyone got out. Loren picked up her dress and her dad helped her up. Paula was right there to fluff out the train and veil. She then took her place to be escorted to the front row where the parents were seated. Gray stood tall beside his daughter. So proud was he to be doing this that he too, shed a tear. Loren saw it and with a gloved hand, brushed it away, smiling at him.

"Dad, I love you."

"I love you, too, Loren. We have come a long way in the past couple of months, haven't we?"

"Yes, dad. I think Mom has too. I think she is reading the Bible. I know you are."

Gray nodded. "Yes, I am. Words can't tell you what you have done to this family. That horseback journey was the best idea you ever had. It has changed your life and look where you are now. You are on the way to become a married woman."

"Oh, dad, you are going to make me cry and ruin my make-up! Oh, they are playing my song! Time to go!"

They walked over to the road leading up toward the minister and Andy. The wedding song was being played. Everyone looked at her and stood up. If she had looked back at the barn, she would have seen Ranger, Brownie and Andy's horse standing at the fence looking on. She had only eyes for the handsome man in the black tux standing beside the minister. Soon, she would be Mrs. Andrew Camfield. Excitement began to build up in her stomach as the butterflies began to flutter. Her mouth became dry and she slowly wiped her tongue across them. She was almost at the front! Taking a deep breath, she stepped up beside Andy. His hand groped for hers and gave it a squeeze. She couldn't feel the sweat because of her gloves, but she knew he was just as nervous as she. The look of love shone in his eyes. With the vows said and the pronouncement of their being husband and wife over, they turned toward each other for the kiss to seal the marriage. Slowly, then, they turned toward the audience as the minister introduced them as Mr. and Mrs. Andrew Camfield.

Andy kissed her again before they started down the aisle. They had done it! They went down the aisle to the guest cabin to wait for everyone to file down and the tables of food set up in the yard. Tomorrow morning they would start their trip on horseback. Tonight, they would stay in the cabin together.

The meal was soon ready and everyone enjoyed the barbeque. The cake was cut and eaten. Guests began to leave soon after some of the gifts were opened. It had been a long day for some of them. They knew the newlyweds wanted to be alone. Joel and Bessie retired to their home. The friends at the Church cleaned up the area and went to their homes. Leftovers were carefully stored in the refrigerator in the barn. Andy put the ice packs for their trip in the freezer. Together they prepared the food for their trip and Joel had already gotten the horse's grain sacked for the three horses. Andy would drive back there after they had gotten settled to get more things for the house and Loren's extra clothes and things from her home. Right now, they were excited about their trip, so much that they couldn't sleep.

Before the weather turned really cold that night, they sat in the porch swing on the cabin's porch. Loren rested in the crook of Andy's arm as they gently rocked in the swing. Silence was golden. The night air was cool on their faces as the many stars in the heavens twinkled far above.

Soon, Loren put a hand over her mouth to cover up a yawn. She was now getting sleepy. Andy took the hint and stood up, pulling her up into his arms.

"Come on, little wife. We need to get to sleep. We have a big day tomorrow."

"Yes, dear." She reached up to ruffle up his hair.

Giggling, she eeked as Andy jabbed a finger into her ribs. In a flash, Loren was sprinting around the yard with Andy right on her heels. Both were laughing like little children. She was snagged around the waist, almost lifting her off her feet. Andy pulled her hard against him, their faces inches apart. His arms like steel bands around her waist.

"Just where do you think you are going, wife?"

"It seems that nowhere, dear sir." Her breathing became ragged as his hands slowly ran up and down her back. She couldn't think. She could feel his breath on her face. So close! Oh, the love she saw in his eyes! Could he see hers?

Andy kissed her, then with his hand in hers, led her back to the cabin where they went inside. The lights were turned off. The busy day was at its end.

Joel's stables was in a whirlwind of activity early the next morning. Andy's horse and pack horse were led out, brushed and prepared to saddle. Ranger neighed, thinking he was being left behind until he saw Loren come for him with a lead rope. He met her at the gate and practically shoved his nose into the halter. The feel of a brush on his back felt good. He wiggled in anticipation of what was coming. He hadn't had a good brushing since they all went riding together several weeks ago.

With the horses saddled and ready, Andy prepared to pack the tent and supplies onto the other horse. Brownie stayed behind to be used as a riding horse for new riders. Joel and Bessie came out with the saddlebags full of food for their trip. Andy tied the last rope tight on the packhorse. He took the saddlebags and tied them behind his saddle. Loren put both rain slickers behind hers along with her saddlebags carrying her Bible and cosmetics. After checking the tightness of the saddle, she walked over to give Joel and Bessie a hug.

"Thanks for everything. We will probably be back in a couple of weeks."

"We'll look forward to that. Bessie can have an apple pie ready."

Andy laughed. "Now, dad, you have to start losing that weight I helped you put on starting now and when we show up again. Don't you go and spoil him, Mom."

"I won't Andy. God bless both of you. Ride carefully."

Both swung into their saddles and turned the horses toward the dirt road leading toward their new home. They were finally alone and married! Their pace was slow even though Ranger kept pulling on the reins to go faster. He didn't know where he was going, but he wanted to go! Loren laughed at him and let him walk at least at a faster pace. If they camped at Andy's old cabin at the valley, then maybe they could have that second run.

Andy hadn't told Loren about the farm in Waverly. That was his big wedding surprise. Sometime in the next couple of days, the wallpaper photograph of the wedding scene should be placed on the wall around the fireplace in their living room. That would really surprise her. Then every day they could look at it and remember the wedding day or the first day they had ridden their horses and found it. Andy looked over at Loren sitting easily in the saddle. So much had happened to them in the last few weeks.

His computer chip sales was up and they could live comfortably close to the life style Loren had been used to. He chewed on his lower lip. Could she really be satisfied with a farmhouse sort of in the country? Would she miss those big department stores where she could shop until she dropped? Time would tell. Right now, she was his and he was going to enjoy her company.

"Andy?"

"Yes, dear."

"Do we still have the cow?"

"Of course. Can't get rid of old Bessie. Why do you ask?"

"I was just wondering if one of my duties as your wife would require milking the cow."

Andy laughed. "Sure. I'll even throw in the cat to catch the milk and you can milk Bessie twice a day. How's that?"

"Wonderful! I love you, Andy."

"Did you hear that, Ranger? He's going to let me milk the cow. And twice a day! Yahooo!"

THE END

Printed in the United States
By Bookmasters